She coul

that poor girl

blonde hair, matted with blood from the inch-deep gash in her throat. The waxy white of her skin meant she'd been dead for a while.

Why had she been dumped here of all places?

Violent crime hardly ever occurred in this town. It had to be a coincidence her farm had been chosen. *Didn't it?*

But deep in her heart, she didn't believe it. *Maybe your past stays with you, no matter how hard you try to leave it behind.*

Rachel knew Seth Talbot had been a New York detective for a couple of years until his hometown lured him back. How much time did she have before he discovered the truth about her? How long before the scorn of the townspeople forced her to move on?

The Daughter of Death

by

Dianne McCartney

The Daughter of Death

Contact Information: info@thewildrosepress.com

Cover Art by *Abigail Owen*

The Wild Rose Press, Inc.
PO Box 708
Adams Basin, NY 14410-0708
Visit us at www.thewildrosepress.com

Publishing History
First Crimson Rose Edition, 2019
Print ISBN 978-1-5092-2731-0
Digital ISBN 978-1-5092-2732-7

Published in the United States of America

Dedication

Thanks to
my wonderful husband, Mitch, and daughter, Colleen,
who are always on the front lines of support,
especially with weird and wonderful computer issues.

Acknowledgments

I owe a great deal to the endless patience and humor of my editor, Ally Robertson, and the rest of the gang at The Wild Rose Press. I couldn't ask for a better support system.

I also want to thank my dear friend MaryAnn Manning, who many years ago suggested a local writing group might be fun and always lent an ear when needed. And thanks to my friend and walking partner Kathy Bird, who always gets excited about my books.

Finally, sending a parting wave to my dad, who died earlier this year at the impressive age of ninety-six.

Chapter One

People in town said Rachel Mann led a simple life and, in that, they didn't lie. For her, a defined routine was not a matter of choice, but an essential. She didn't bother to explain her reasoning—the dialogue required more personal contact than she desired.

At 6:05 a.m. Rachel headed out onto her deck, pulling on her fleece jacket to ward off the early morning chill. Her boots made a hollow thud on the thick cedar planks as she stopped to survey the surrounding beauty. She gazed at the most compelling reason for buying this property two years ago—twenty-five acres of land spread in all directions with no other houses in sight. Solitude proved a precious commodity.

The early Tennessee autumn had coaxed a few reluctant leaves to turn. In a couple of weeks, a flood of color would tempt artists and photographers to stop by the roadside and snap dozens of pictures. She posted No Trespassing signs on her property at regular intervals to keep the most persistent observers away.

She stepped off the bottom stair. The dogs appeared, tongues lolling, brothers, part Labrador, that some thoughtless moron had dumped in a box at the end of the drive. She lacked a hard-enough heart to turn them out. Almost two years old now and as big as houses, she'd named them Jack and Zack, but called them "you two" more often than not, as they stuck together like burrs to wool.

Used to the ritual, they trailed after her as she struck off. She set a brisk pace, enjoying the slap of cold air against her cheeks. An hour spent crowning the tops of the surrounding hills might give her an appetite for breakfast.

Halfway through their walk, Jack growled. She stopped in her tracks, watching, puzzled, as the hair on his back formed a ridge along his spine. "What's wrong?" she asked, walking to lay a hand on his head. He shot ahead of her, racing down the hill to a shadowed gully under the trees.

"Jack!" She jogged after him, wondering what had spooked him and hoping to find another dog, rather than a bear. Zack raced past her to catch up with his brother.

They stood, their backs to her, in a typical investigative pose, their noses pressed to the ground, tails quivering. A flash of purple caught her eye, and moving closer, she saw a jacket lying on the ground.

Then she saw a form under the jacket.

Air she drew into her lungs seemed eager to leave. Her legs threatened to give, and she shut her eyes for a moment to gather strength. Forcing herself to move forward, she took a closer look, praying some drunk from town had simply helped himself to nature's bed.

Her prayers went unanswered.

One shocked look told Rachel the young woman had passed the point where help could come quickly enough. The gaping gash in her throat no longer oozed blood; the smears had dried on her ghost-white skin. "Come here," Rachel said to the dogs and, hearing the tremble in her voice, patted the side of her leg for emphasis. They came reluctantly, their dark eyes questioning.

"Home," she said, and they moved off with her, one on either side, instead of bounding ahead. She didn't think she needed a guard, but the positions they chose gave her pause.

Rachel tried not to think of the painful repercussions of what would come next. The poor girl in the glen had suffered more than she, herself, would. But could she act as a normal person would under these circumstances? Anything else might raise questions. Questions she had to avoid at all costs.

She hurried to the phone, yanking off her gloves, and with shaky fingers, dialed the sheriff's number. She reached him in person, solely by her stubborn refusal to talk to anyone else. "This is Rachel Mann speaking. You need to come up to my place right away."

Seth Talbot, his voice low and steady, asked, "What's going on? Are you okay?"

"I have a dead body in my field. It's a young woman. You need to come right now." She hung up as his voice sharpened in response.

Rachel locked the dogs in her bedroom to prevent them from getting underfoot. Her rolling stomach forced her to stop for a glass of water. The sheriff's office was located just a ten-minute drive away—he'd make it in less this morning, she figured. She closed her eyes and tried for a calming breath. *Why me? I can't go through this again.*

Securing the door behind her, she waited at the bottom of the steps. After a few minutes, she saw the telltale dust that signaled the sheriff's imminent arrival and watched his speedy entry in between the two towering trees that marked her driveway.

He jolted to a stop in front of her and swung long, muscled legs out the door. Seth Talbot looked like an advertisement for testosterone—tall, broad, and dark. No doubt the women in town found his type attractive. He pulled off his sunglasses. "Is there any chance you're mistaken?"

"No."

"Then you'd better show me."

He opened the passenger door and waved her to take a seat. Reluctantly, she did. They bumped across the field in his car until the hill began to slope to the gully. "Stop here," she instructed. Wrenching open the door, Rachel slammed it and struck off at a brisk pace, knowing he could keep up.

Seth stayed abreast. "When did you find the body?"

"Right before I called you. What—did you think I stopped to have breakfast?"

His stare made it clear she was out of line.

"Look, I'm a little rattled, okay?" She slowed a bit. "I went out for my morning walk, and the dogs went on alert about halfway down the hill. She's lying in the gully."

"Did you check her pulse?"

Her stomach heaved. She hung on with grim resolve. "I didn't have to. She's been dead a while."

Seth frowned. "How can you be sure?"

"I'm sure." She swallowed. "I think she's been dead a while."

"Did the dogs get at her?"

Rachel shook her head. "They just stood beside her and sniffed. When I saw what was lying there, I called them off."

They reached the edge of the glen where sunlight transitioned into shadow. He slowed when he absorbed what waited there and cursed, reaching for the radio strapped on his hip. "Rosie, it's me. We have a body, so we'll need the coroner here, asap. And send over anybody else that's not tied up. We're on the southeast side of her property, at the bottom of the hill."

He told Rachel to take a seat close to the car and she did as directed, sitting cross-legged, grateful to feel the cool, firm ground underneath her. Before long, the coroner's van reached them, accompanied by two deputies who, according to the looks on their faces, had never seen a murder victim. They roped off a large area around the body with crime scene tape, and the sheriff snarled when they wandered too close.

Seth took dozens of pictures from the camera he kept in his car. After what seemed an eternity, they removed the corpse. Doc Vernon conferred with the sheriff and then left, giving her a somber nod as he passed. Rachel felt ashamed by the relief she felt as the van drove off.

The sheriff squatted down beside her. "We didn't recognize her. Do you?"

She shook her head.

"Looks to be in her early to mid-twenties." He gave her a considering look. "The murder didn't happen here, you know. Somebody dropped her off."

"I know."

Seth raised a questioning eyebrow.

"Well, those injuries didn't look very fresh, and she wasn't here on my evening walk."

His gaze sharpened, and for the first time, she

noticed the laser blue intensity of his eyes. "When was that?"

"I leave the house at 6:05 morning and night, every day, so I'd guess about 6:20."

"Do you always follow the same path?"

Rachel nodded. "Close enough."

"And you're sure you would have noticed?"

She tried hard not to be insulted. "Yes. And I always have the dogs with me. They would have caught the scent even if I hadn't."

Seth nodded. "Well, that'll help with the time frame anyway." He stood and she joined him, heading up hill. "Are you going to be in for the rest of the day?"

It was a rhetorical question, and they both knew it. The fact that she seldom left her property made good gossip for idle minds. "Yes, I'll be here."

"I'm sorry you have to be saddled with this."

He sounded as if he meant it. "It's not your fault."

"I'll likely have some more questions later, but if you think of anything that might help in the meantime, call me." He handed her a card. "Here are the numbers for both my office and my private line. Call anytime."

Rachel watched him as she climbed the steps, turning sideways to see him pick up the radio and talk into it. The car didn't move as she let herself into the house. Finally, he climbed into his car and trailed after the others, down the long hill and back onto the county road.

When she let the dogs out of their room, they circled anxiously around her legs, growling at the sight of the departing car. They forgot about it as soon as she fed them, gulping down the dry food with all the finesse of starving teenagers.

She couldn't summon any appetite. The picture of that poor girl kept swimming into her vision—the pale blonde hair, matted with blood from the inch-deep gash in her throat. The waxy white of her skin meant she'd been dead for a while.

Why had she been dumped here of all places?

Violent crime hardly ever occurred in this town. It had to be a coincidence her farm had been chosen. *Didn't it?*

But deep in her heart, she didn't believe it. *Maybe your past stays with you, no matter how hard you try to leave it behind.*

Rachel knew Seth Talbot had been a New York detective for a couple of years until his hometown lured him back. How much time did she have before he discovered the truth about her? How long before the scorn of the townspeople forced her to move on?

Chapter Two

Seth thought he left all this mayhem behind him when he moved back from the Big Apple. In the two years he'd been sheriff, there had been no murders at all. In towns this size, the most excitement they experienced was the occasional car wreck or domestic call. Seth had seen enough death to last a lifetime.

He'd sent the initial details about this morning's victim to all the surrounding counties to see if they had a missing person that matched. The only missing person in town was Elmer Tate, who went missing every two weeks when his paycheck came in. He'd hightail it off with his buddies for a binge and his long-suffering wife would come in and weep all over Seth's collar. Seth didn't figure Elmer counted as a missing person.

Doc guessed the young woman had been dead two to three days and had promised him a full report by nightfall. Seth noted the cut in the girl's neck had been deep and jagged, implying strength and a lack of finesse, but at this point he didn't have anything else. His four deputies stayed busy checking with all the neighbors to see if anyone had seen a strange vehicle in the area.

One of Rachel's neighbors, Hooky Hobart, said he wouldn't be surprised if Rachel Mann hadn't done it herself. When Seth asked why he thought so, the idiot replied that she was "unnatural," living up there herself.

At that point, Seth decided to leave the neighbors to the deputies to question. He'd bet a dime to a dollar Hobart had tried to pull a fast move on Rachel. Imagining her response made him grin for the first time all day. No, Seth was a pretty good judge of people. Rachel might be a loner, and prickly at times, but she'd been shaken by this recent turn of events. He knew that much.

Of course, by the time all was said and done, he would have to look at damn near everyone in town if he had a hope of finding the killer. His radio crackled to life. "Sheriff?" It was the sincere and squeaky voice of Wayne Hiscock, his youngest deputy. Appearances can be deceptive; he was undoubtedly the smartest of the four deputies.

"Yes, Wayne."

His voice struggled through the static. "Amos Green says he saw a black truck stopped on the back road behind his place just before midnight. Said he was gonna call you about it when he got up this mornin', but it was gone by then."

"All right. Are you at Amos's house?"

"Yes."

"You and Amos stay put. I'll come and get you and see if we can hunt up a track."

"We'll be waitin'."

Normally the drive to Amos's place would make any fool smile, just from seeing the rich, green grass and the hearty apple trees that bloomed alongside his driveway. But today hadn't started off well and was unlikely to get much better.

The kind of man who made Seth's job easy, Amos farmed and tended his well-behaved children and affectionate wife even better than he did his beloved crops. But today, as Seth approached the cheery red and white outbuildings, he saw the saddened expression on the farmer's face as he stood waiting with Wayne. Amos pulled his shoulders back as Seth approached and rubbed one hand into his graying beard. "This is an awful thing we have here."

Seth nodded. "Do you think you can show me where this truck was parked?"

"Yes." Amos walked around to the passenger door of the cruiser and climbed in. Almost too tall to fit, Wayne hopped in the back, folding his legs so his knees almost hit the top of the front seat.

Seth took the much shorter back drive, which led out onto an old farm road now used mostly by the people whose properties adjoined it. Amos began to speak. "I drove home from my brother's, passed here just before midnight. Wasn't anybody in the truck. I looked." He shrugged. "Figured somebody must have broken down."

"What make?"

"Chevy, a few years old, at least. Just a plain old black truck. Nothin' fancy." He peered through the glass. " 'Bout another twenty yards now, I'd say."

Seth eased to a stop twenty feet away from the spot Amos indicated. "You two just stay in the car a minute and let me have a look." He slid out and advanced toward the spot Amos had indicated. There wouldn't be any track here, he saw with disappointment, not at this spot, where dirt gave way to crushed stone. The only sign someone had stopped there was a slight banking of the gravel, as if the truck had gone a bit too far onto the soft shoulder. And he counted on the fact that Amos hadn't made a mistake about the location.

Looking up, he saw the sight line with Rachel's property was perfect. He remembered a beaten path that wound through the trees, just a little to the left. It had offered the perfect make-out spot for high school kids, close to town, but private.

He went back to the car. "Wayne, I'm going to take some tape and a camera. You run Amos home, then come on back and give me a hand."

"You think the truck had that girl as cargo?" Amos's expression showed he already knew the answer.

Seth nodded.

"Christ, save us." Amos wiped a hand across his eyes. "I should have stopped."

Seth knew the man well enough to know he was thinking of his own children and of the parents who would be getting bad news any minute. "It wouldn't have helped, Amos. This information will get out sooner or later anyway, so I'll tell you, but keep it to yourself for now. You couldn't have saved her. It was already too late."

"Poor child."

Seth retrieved his supplies from the trunk and watched as the other two men departed. Turning, he looked upwards, where the roof of Rachel's house showed through the trees. He'd have to stop in and see her again when he was done, and wouldn't she be pleased about that.

An hour later, he arranged for one of the other deputies to come and pick up Wayne to drop him back at his car so they could both head home for the day. He continued on to Rachel's. The dogs set up a chorus of howls when he stopped at her front steps. She met him on the deck as if determined to keep him outside.

"Can I come in for a minute?"

Her dark, suspicious eyes gave him the once-over twice. Without answering, she turned and went through the door. That it stayed open for him proved invitation enough.

The dogs bounced and wiggled at his feet, and he stopped to give them each a pat. "Some guard dogs you are," he muttered and earned himself another of Rachel's steely looks. She gestured to a chair.

The pretty kitchen surprised him. It appeared much warmer than she did, with terracotta floors and comfy golden oak chairs. The dimming light of early evening couldn't hide the fact that everything looked pin neat as his mother used to say.

"What do you want?"

Her lack of hospitality energized him more than anything else. "Amos Green saw a black truck on the back road about midnight. I was wondering if you might have noticed it."

"I go to bed at ten."

Seth considered her answer. *Interesting. Not around ten, or usually ten, but "at ten."* He figured she'd moved past scheduled and into compulsive. "And you didn't see this truck around earlier in the evening?"

"No. I saw Amos's light blue truck and that idiot Hobart's rig, but that's it."

He settled back into his chair, delaying his exit just to annoy her. "You and Hobart don't get along?"

"The man's an orangutan."

The description was so apt he chuckled. "Now, that's not too neighborly, although probably well deserved." He sobered. "He wasn't too complimentary about you, either."

"Oh, I'll spend the rest of my life worrying about that." She dusted her hands off on her jeans. "Was there anything else?"

She's not at all subtle, is she? "Yes. I'd like to walk your share of the pasture path if that's okay."

"You don't need my permission." Without even a pause, she winced. "Sorry. Do whatever you need to do."

He stretched his legs and stood. "I appreciate that."

Seth could feel her stare on the back of his head as he made his way down the steps. Rachel reminded him of a wounded bear who just wanted to be left alone. Who knows where the wounds came from? It really wasn't any of his business.

There were cattle on the five acres that adjoined Amos's property. According to Amos, she let him use it in exchange for mowing her fields. Seth left his car at the top of the hill where he had parked that morning. Rachel's property ended just past where the body had been found, the line made visible by the sudden surge of overgrown grass and brush. He traced the likely path, irritated because the lack of rain helped a murderer avoid leaving footprints.

Ten minutes brought him nothing but more frustration, then he caught sight of a paper weighted down by a rock, just off the path. The rock balanced on the upper edge of a boulder. Premonition made him slip on the latex gloves he kept in his pocket.

Folded over, the lined paper looked as if it had been torn from a student's spiral notebook. Seth eased the rock to one side and lifted the edges of his find with two fingers. He wedged it open to read the words, written in a blur of what looked like colored pencil.

Ain't she pretty? There're dozens more where she came from.

As soon as Seth read those words, he knew they weren't going to see the end of these killings anytime soon.

****

Rachel paced in the house, hiding the binoculars behind her back when Seth trudged up the hill, as if he could see through the walls. She wondered what he had found down there in the rocks. A flash of white, probably paper, that he tucked into an evidence bag. He'd hunted around for another twenty minutes, but appeared to come up short in terms of finding anything else.

Amos had already called and told her about the truck. Poor man, he seemed to take the weight of the world on his shoulders, as if he were somehow responsible for the murder of that girl.

She doubted she would learn much from Seth about the investigation, but word would soon swirl through town if they discovered the girl's identity. It could be a love affair gone bad or just a simple botched robbery, but it didn't feel like either one.

Standard procedure in these cases included checking the background of everyone involved if only to rule them out. She tried to imagine where her name might appear on that rather short list and when Seth might come knocking on her door with more questions than she wanted to answer.

Rachel waited until Seth's car disappeared through the gates, then let the dogs out again. Standing at the window she watched them play, debating whether these circumstances would force her to give up this acreage and move on again. Out of all the places she'd lived, and there had been many, this was the location she loved the best. The land suited her, the rolling hills and thick, tall trees. The isolation of these twenty-five acres proved a restorative to her trampled spirit.

Rachel didn't choose anything out of the refrigerator for supper. The thought of that poor girl stole her appetite. The plaintive mooing of the cows and the dogs barking in a playful tone some distance away registered as she entered the den.

Books lined every wall of the spacious room. They made reliable company. Her computer and business files were out of sight in the second bedroom. She knew the townspeople questioned how she earned a living. Like everything else, it was none of their business. A perverse part of her speculated on how they would feel if they knew she owned several stores and one restaurant in this town. The ownership stayed hidden beneath a maze of paperwork. The day-to-day dealings of each one held no interest for her as long as they continued to make a generous profit that allowed her to live as she wished.

Her typical workday lasted only about three or four hours, done totally by computer. It permitted her to spend the rest of her time as she wished, engrossed in books, working on her property, and playing with the dogs. She tried never to think of the past, although sometimes fear snuck into her dreams and forced her to spend the night pacing until the sun came up.

Rachel never bothered thinking about the future either, figuring it would come, regardless.

Chapter Three

When Rachel started out for her walk the next morning, she found Seth on her driveway, squatting to pat her dogs. She tried not to growl her hello.

"Morning." He straightened and smiled. "I hope you don't mind. You said you're an early riser, and I have a few questions."

"I was heading for my walk."

He nodded. "Thought I'd just come along, if that's all right."

What choice do I have? She struck out, and he kept pace as the dogs rushed ahead. "Did you learn anything about the girl?"

"We have three possibilities in the whole state. We'll rule them out before we look any further."

They continued in silence, then Seth slowed a little. "Do you have any enemies, Rachel?"

"This doesn't have anything to do with me."

"How do you know?"

She tried to walk on, but he caught her arm and pulled her to a stop. Jack came racing back, stopping to give an uncertain growl. "Off, Jack. I'm okay." The dog left again after a final proprietary glance.

Seth released her. "Maybe they're better guard dogs than I thought." He studied her face for a minute. "How can you be sure this has nothing to do with you?"

"Because it doesn't make any sense." She

struggled to moderate her tone. “I mind my own business. I pay my bills. I don’t bother anyone.”

An incredulous look came over his face. “I wasn’t implying you deserve to be involved. I’m trying to look at every angle I can, because I have almost nothing to work with here.”

“You found something last night.”

His eyes zeroed in on hers. “I’ll ask you to keep that to yourself.”

Who am I going to tell? My dogs? “Will there be more killings, do you think?”

Rachel read the answer on his face, even though he responded, “I don’t know.”

They resumed walking and then he spoke. “Have you had any threats recently?”

Define recently. She swallowed the impulse to say that out loud. “No.”

“No spurned lovers or psychotic ex-husbands?”

She stifled a groan, although she understood the questions were an integral part of his job. “Neither. I’m pretty boring, as almost anyone in town would be happy to inform you.”

“You can’t think of any reason the killer chose your farm as the dumping ground?”

She schooled her expression to its usual frigid calm. “No. Not a thing.” All the while, she wondered if Seth could hear her knees clattering together or see into the fractured remnants of her heart. *Does he believe me?*

Seth knew one thing as he drove away—Rachel was hiding something. Not guilt, but fear had slipped into her eyes before sheer control managed to remove it. Of course, any sane woman would be frightened under the circumstances, but he suspected there might be more to it than that. He continued to mull it over on his way to the station, only stopping to help Miss Eunice get her cat out of the tree again.

His assistant, Rosie, was away from her desk. When Seth opened the door to his office, he found his oldest deputy, Brady Doss, his boots propped up on the desk. Seth's glare brought them off with a thud. Brady wore his usual smirk, though, along with his rumpled uniform. "Just thought I'd check in, see what's going on today."

"Didn't you read the duty roster?"

Brady laughed. "Yeah, but it had me on patrol."

"That's right."

His statement brought a frown. "I figured you'd need me with you on this other big deal."

Seth shook his head. "Wayne's working it with me. I need you to take care of patrol."

"I've been here longer," Brady whined. "Wayne's just a kid—he doesn't have my experience."

"Last time I checked, I was in charge here." The tension hung in the air between them until Brady left, bitching under his breath.

This is what happened when you did a friend a favor. The mayor had begged Seth to keep his nephew Brady on as deputy when Seth landed the job, but now he regretted it. He made more work than he took care of with his dumbass remarks and nonexistent work ethic.

It didn't help that his twice-married deputy thought he was a major stud and annoyed the hell out of most women. Seth had seen him out on the town one night, in a silk shirt undone to his waist and too-tight jeans. He looked like a seventies leftover—too bad disco days were done.

A glance at his watch told him 7:30 a.m. might be too early to start calling in some favors. He needed a discreet background check done on Rachel. It might also be necessary to goose the other departments that promised to send him the information on those three missing girls. He hoped it turned out to be one of the three. If not, a nationwide check would become necessary, and that took time. Seth didn't know how much time he had before the killer struck again.

Rosie had sent a package containing the note to a forensic lab in the city he'd used in the past. Hopefully they could tell him something, anything, that would give him some kind of an edge.

Doc Vernon came up with the time of death being approximately forty-eight hours before she was found. That gave someone plenty of time to drive her in from almost anywhere. Doc also said the weapon used was likely the blade from lawn shears. The cut had been awkward, the blade unusually thick.

She had been raped, repeatedly, but although there were numerous abrasions, there was no blood or semen found. The lack of DNA was frustrating. After the murder, the killer carefully re-dressed her, panties and all. Last night Seth submitted the details to the nationwide network, looking for similar crimes. No luck there, not yet anyway.

Rosie bustled in the door, wearing her perpetual smile and yet another sunny yellow skirt, complemented by dangling, happy face earrings. "Morning, boss. This just came in." Thank goodness for upbeat people. There were already too many of the other kind.

He took two sheets of paper from her grasp, and with a glance, saw that the first missing person information had arrived. Someone was on the ball. "Great. No sign of the others yet?"

She tsked-tsked up at him from her height a foot below his own. "Not even eight o'clock, Seth. They'll be along." She shut the door herself, her dark, wavy hair floating behind her.

Seth scanned the sheet. Karen Anders, twenty-one, missing three months. The photo showed her to be a pretty girl with shoulder-length blonde hair. At five feet six, the height matched and her build was similar, but Seth didn't think this was the one. Her nose, he realized, looked longer than his victim, her ears a little bigger. He'd take it to Doc anyway, just to be sure.

It was a tragic thing when your best-case scenario involved selecting which family to notify by nightfall.

****

Rachel felt too restless to work. She'd sat down at the computer three different times, then given up in disgust. The clock showed it was nearly noon, and she had nothing to show for it except a headache.

A knock on the door interrupted her thoughts. She glanced out a side window to see Amos. Embarrassed because the knock jangled her nerves, she opened the door. "Good morning."

He wiped his feet and followed her back inside. "Just wanted to check in, make sure you're doin' all right."

"I'm okay." She poured him a mug of coffee and placed it on the counter next to him, knowing he wouldn't take the time to sit. "How are Edith and the children?"

"Edith's a mite upset. Doesn't want to let the girls out of her sight. The boys are all primed to help the sheriff investigate."

The boys were four, twelve and fourteen, respectively, and like most of their generation watched too much television. To Amos's dismay, none of them had inherited his love of the land or at least hadn't shown any signs of it thus far. "Do you think the killer might be someone local?" As soon as the words escaped, she realized how stupid that sounded.

Amos shook his head. "I hope not. To be honest with you, Rachel, the idea scares the bejesus out of me. That's a good part of the reason we live out here, to be clear of this kind of thing."

"How else would he know about the path?"

"I don't know. I'm havin' a hard time believing such a thing could happen here, of all places." He rubbed bent fingers through his beard. "You still got that gun?"

Rachel nodded, remembering how she'd checked it twice last night. "Yes." She tried to smile and make him relax. "I'm hoping I won't need it, of course."

Grimacing, he took a few sips of coffee. "Edith and me, we worry about you up here by yourself."

Rachel felt a lump in her throat. He and his family were the only people who gave a damn.

"If you're concerned about anything, even during the night, you call now."

She tried a smile to reassure him. "Don't worry, Amos. The dogs will keep me safe."

But even she didn't really believe that.

That night, she dreamt not of her father, as expected, but of her mother. Renee's dark eyes stared, ringed with sorrow, on the last night Rachel had ever seen her. She remembered, on that morning, her mother held her a little too close. In response, Rachel had pulled away, asking why she needed to leave. Afterward, in memory, the scene always proceeded in slow motion as her mother walked out the door, stopping just long enough to take one final, tearful look back. That last glance branded itself on Rachel's memory, not the happy times of her childhood, but a horrible certainty life would never be the same.

Rachel waited and waited for her mother to return. There was little food in the house, but Rachel had no appetite to balance the gnawing fear. Two days later, a policewoman showed up at the house and took her away. They said her mother had gone to heaven.

Gone to heaven to escape hell, Rachel realized.

She spent the three months before her eighteenth birthday at a foster home. The nameless, faceless people offered food and a bed which was all she needed. The day she turned eighteen, she left with a backpack of her meager belongings and never returned.

Frustrated with the lingering memories, Rachel rose from the bed, pushing back the wild tangle of her hair. She ran a battered brush through the snarl—the dogs wouldn't care about any morning beauty routine.

If variety was the spice of life, Rachel qualified as spiceless. Glancing at the clock, she headed for the door, pulling on a jacket. Six-o-four—the dogs would be waiting. Tongues lolling, they gave her their version of a good morning grin, tails beating the air like two brooms against a dusty rug. She whistled to them, and they all set off on their stroll.

A flash of color caught her eye, and Rachel

stopped, recognizing the sheriff's car down on the main road. He cruised past, taking his time, and then she heard the beep of its horn. Feeling forced to respond, she raised a hand in a half-hearted salute and continued on her way.

She felt pinned under a microscope, knowing Seth's eyes would be on her as she set off on her walk. *Shouldn't I feel better that he's keeping an eye on the place?* Still, the very thought of his constant observation, or anybody else's for that matter, agitated her.

A sense of childish denial made her want to avoid the murder site, but she made herself look down into the hollow where the body had lain. A slip of paper lay there, anchored on the spot. She blinked a few times, then stared at it, willing herself to believe a random piece of garbage had blown her way. Inching closer, she could see the edges flutter in the breeze. She didn't venture any farther, because she could glimpse the suggestion of printed words against the white.

Damn it.

This time she jogged back to the house. She didn't have to place another dreaded phone call—the sheriff had circled around and sped his way up the drive. He hurried out of the car, the door slamming the air with unwelcome sound. "What's wrong?"

"A note," she puffed. "I didn't touch it, but it's right in that same place where he left the body."

"Shit." Seth waved her into his vehicle, and they drove to the top of the hill with the dogs trotting after them, stopping at the crest. He opened his trunk to withdraw the same kit he'd used the previous day. "You're sure you didn't touch it?"

She glared. "Of course. I'm not an idiot. I stayed twenty feet away."

"Good girl." He pulled on a pair of gloves, giving the approaching dogs a glance. "Keep them out of the way."

She frowned at him, then turned to face the dogs. "Go home." They lumbered off, reluctance evident in their drooping tails as they headed for the house.

"They're pretty well trained."

She nodded and followed him down the hill, stopping when he gestured. "Stay here."

Rachel did as she was told, which went against the grain. Watching with growing unease as he worked, she half expected him to tease her about a piece of trash having landed in that place.

It didn't happen. He scanned the ground as he searched the site, twice squatting on his heels to study the grass. He pulled the camera out of his kit, took a few pictures, then his slim fingers grasped the edge of the paper, carefully moving the two anchoring stones. He read for a moment, then his frown of concentration turned grim.

"What does it say?"

Seth scowled at her but didn't respond. He reached into his pocket and withdrew a plastic bag, folding the note and easing it inside.

She opened her mouth to repeat her question, but he beat her to it.

"Why you?"

The question caught her by surprise. "What do you mean?"

"Why do you think he focused on your home?"

She felt tension creep through her gut. "What did

the note say?"

He stared, as if he could see into her soul. "I shouldn't tell you. What if you repeat it to someone?"

That ridiculous concern almost caused a hysterical giggle. She knew how to keep a secret—the one thing at which she excelled. "I won't."

He stopped beside her, glaring down. "It says 'Why does a beautiful woman like you live here alone? Aren't you worried about what waits for you in the dark?' "

His words caused her to sway, and he reached out a hand to steady her. "Rachel," Seth said, gripping her arm. "Is there something I should know?"

Reveal nothing. She grappled for some restraint. "I don't know anything about this." But darkness pursued her, constantly. *How does this monster know that?*

Rachel yanked her arm away. "I shouldn't have bothered you. This is just some high school dropout's idea of playing with the local freak." She started up the hill, and he followed.

"What kind of protection do you have?"

Not enough, she thought. *Never enough*. "I have a gun and two very protective dogs." She intuited his next question. "And yes, I have a concealed carry permit."

"Do you really know how to shoot or do you plan to shut your eyes and hope for the best?"

The sarcasm in his voice spurred her on. "I can shoot that arrogant nose right off your face at fifty yards. Is that good enough for you?"

"I guess it'll have to do." He increased his stride to match hers.

Rachel continued to stomp past his car.

"Where the hell are you going? I'll drive you

back."

She whirled to face him. "I'm quite damn able to walk my own damn self back to my own damn house. Just do your job." Fury propelled her almost to the steps before he passed her, driving fast enough to spit gravel in her direction.

So, Sheriff Perfect has a temper, does he?

Tough shit.

Chapter Four

That woman would make a priest turn to Satan, Seth thought as he struggled to regain his temper. He slowed the car, exiting through the gates. Rachel reminded him of an injured cat, hissing and spitting if you ventured too close.

But he'd recognized fear in those dark eyes as he read her the note. People responded differently to threats, as he had discovered during the course of his career. Some clung and others resorted to anger. He figured lashing out would always be the simplest course for Rachel.

Seth couldn't for the life of him figure out why she intrigued him. He mulled over that problem as he made his way back to the office, gesturing for Rosie to join him. "How's the background check on Rachel Mann coming?"

"You should have something by late afternoon."

"Give them a little prod to make sure we do."

Rosie sent him an assessing look. "Do you really think she has something to do with this?"

"To be honest with you, Rosie, I'm worried she's square in the receiving end of trouble." He filled his assistant in about the note and passed it to her. "Get this off to the lab asap."

"Sure, Seth."

"One more thing."

Rosie perched on the edge of his desk, one eyebrow raised.

"You're more observant than most. What's your impression of Rachel?"

Rosie pursed her lips. "Proud, independent, a bit cranky. But also, sad and a little lonely."

"Sad?"

She nodded. "There's a pensive quality about her, as if she wished she could just slide into the horizon." With that rather profound statement, his assistant inched her behind off his desk.

"Have you heard of any men hanging around her?"

Rosie turned toward him, stroking an imaginary mustache. "What is the nature of your interest, boss?" His answering growl hurried her on. "No. There's a lot of talk about how weird it is that there's never been anyone as far as we could tell. A few have tried, only to get shot down in a heartbeat. Amos has a worship from afar type of thing for her, though."

That stunned him. "Amos?" *Good old, God-fearing Amos?*

Rosie chuckled. "Don't look so shocked. He'd never do a damn thing about it, and his wife knows it. He contents himself with the good neighbor role."

She closed the door behind her, leaving Seth to ponder how much more gossip Rosie picked up than ever wandered his way. Someone like Rosie, who people gossiped to, but who knew how to keep her mouth shut, proved an invaluable resource for a small-town department like this one.

Late that afternoon, the initial report came in on Rachel. Seth stared at the closed folder for a moment, then made himself comfortable in his office chair and dug in. He worked backwards, his own peculiar habit, noting ten moves in the last sixteen years, which seemed like a lot. Then he came to a legal name change form.

Why would Rachel need a name change?

People usually altered their names for two reasons; either for business or to create distance from an unwanted segment of their life. He checked the dates. Rachel had been eighteen when she filed the change and was now thirty-four years of age.

At this point, Seth found a note from Rosie. It read, "The investigator asked if you wanted the childhood stuff, too." Picking up the phone, he answered in the affirmative, then returned to the report. He often wondered how Rachel made her living and was surprised to see she owned majority shares in several businesses, a few of them here in town. He knew she didn't take an active hand in their operation and bet the staff didn't know who owned them.

Rachel had a finance degree. That explained how she knew to handle money. Her very healthy bank balance spoke of sound financial management and she had paid off the sizeable mortgage on her property.

She had never married—there went his theory of a love gone wrong. At least she had been honest about that fact.

So, why does a healthy, attractive woman choose to live a life of isolation? Maybe the expected report on her childhood would yield some answers.

****

Rachel sat on the steps, tossing the ball for the dogs to squabble over. The workday ended as it started, a total write-off, thanks to her preoccupation with the murder. She'd tried to look over some business reports, but the print faded away to reveal the distraught young woman, forever frozen between Rachel's back field and eternity. *Will it be better or worse when we learn her name?*

She saw Amos lurch over the brow of the hill, the able red tractor chugging through the thick and thin of the pasture. No one in the county spent as much time as Amos did with his equipment. He could fix anything with an engine. The racket became louder as he headed her way and then throttled it down to a mumble. "Everything okay, Rachel?"

She nodded. "Want some coffee?"

"No, thanks. I'm 'bout to head in for supper. You're welcome to join us if you like."

Rachel never accepted these frequent invitations, but she thought it nice he still bothered to ask. She answered as she always did. "I've already eaten, but thanks for asking." The blatant lie suited them both.

"Saw the sheriff here this morning." Speculation gave his quiet face some light.

She shrugged. "He found some more evidence, I guess."

"Word in town is that the murderer left a note promisin' more trouble."

Bad news travels fast. "Where did you hear that?"

Amos ducked his head, but his ears reddened. "Wife heard it at the beauty parlor. Might not even be true—I hope it's not, anyway." He shifted in the seat and wiped some sweat from his forehead. "You see anything that doesn't look right, be sure to call."

"I will." When he grabbed the wheel, she couldn't help a last-minute plea. "Keep an eye on the kids,

Amos. You never really know what's around."

He nodded. "I'll take care of what's mine. Don't worry."

She watched his progress over the hill, amused as his black and white Holstein cattle followed him as if he were a new-age Pied Piper. The dogs finally tuckered out at sunset and collapsed on the stoop for a nap. She left them there and went inside to read.

The howling woke her around midnight. Rachel jerked awake, adrenaline goosing her heart rate as she realized she'd fallen asleep in the easy chair.

Where are the dogs?

Then the sound came again—a symphony of anguish and alarm.

She ran to the closet, jerked down the nine-millimeter pistol. With one practiced slap of her hand, she loaded the magazine of bullets and headed for the front door.

Call Seth.

And tell him what? That my dogs are barking? He already thought—well, God knows what he thought.

Shoving her bare feet into sneakers, she didn't take time to tie them and turned on the front lights. A preliminary look through the window revealed nothing, but sheer black.

Rachel stepped out onto the porch, her pistol at her side. "Jack, Zack. Come!" They answered with a sound stuck between a bark and a howl, their voices coming closer. She went into a shooting stance, then out of it when the dogs whirled out of the darkness, running pell-mell to meet her. Keeping her back to the house, she opened the door. "In!"

They obeyed at warp speed, as if the night nipped

at their tails. She followed them after one last look. “What’s going on, guys?”

They milled around her legs, more hyper than usual, pushing their heads against her fingers. Their repeated trips to the window worried her, so she shut the drapes as if that would help.

Then the cellphone rang.

Her heartbeat picked up speed again. No one ever called her this late.

She lifted it, swiping. “Hello?”

Amos’ voice asked her if she had trouble.

Some of the reactionary quivers left. “The dogs raised a racket, but it might have been a rabbit. I’m sorry they bothered you.” Rachel reassured him again she’d locked all her doors and hung up. She imagined his concern didn’t endear him to his wife, but she had other things to worry about. Like whether someone lurked outside or she was just being paranoid. She thought of that old joke about even paranoid people getting followed sometimes. It didn’t seem so funny right now.

The dogs never raised that much fuss over rabbits and such. They were far too easygoing, despite her boasting to Seth about having guardians.

So, what had caused them to create a ruckus?

Because of that and all the other questions plaguing her, she spent the rest of the hours before dawn propped in the recliner, one quick arm’s reach away from the gun.

****

Seth thumped his desk in frustration, gaining nothing but a bruise on his hand. Amos had reported a minor disturbance that had happened during the night.

Apparently, his dogs and Rachel's had set to howling, but Amos hadn't called, because nothing seemed to be wrong.

Normally, Seth would have to agree. But it hadn't been a normal week and these were all well-behaved animals, not given to running wild. *Damn Rachel and her stubborn hide.* At least Amos had checked up on her, but Seth still wished she had called.

Decision made, he rose from his chair. He would go and discuss the importance of being vigilant. Grabbing his keys, he opened the door and almost ran Rosie over.

"Slow down," she said, reaching out in a halting motion. "You need to see this."

He waved toward his desk. "Leave it back there. I have to run an errand."

"No," she answered, planting herself square in his path. "You're going to want to take a look, boss."

"What is it?" He didn't try to hide his impatience.

"It's the rest of the report on Rachel Mann." Her expression showed concern. "And it's a doozy. I won't show it to the others until you tell me what to do."

That stopped him in his tracks. Rosie wasn't an alarmist. She left him alone with the paperwork, hadn't even bothered with a folder this time. That meant it had come hot off the presses, so to speak, and required immediate attention.

Premonition slowed his movements. He read the few paragraphs, and whistling in a breath, read them again. He pondered his alternatives, only to discover he had none.

If Rachel had found him an unwelcome guest before, she would hardly welcome him when he came armed to the teeth with her secrets.

He spent all morning and half the afternoon phoning her and running by her place. She and the dogs were nowhere to be found. Anxiety prompted a visit to Amos, who said he'd seen her in the far pasture around lunchtime.

Seth returned to her place as the sun set, watching from a distance as she traipsed home from across the north pasture. His usual good manners took a back seat. "Where the hell have you been?" He crossed his arms and waited for an answer.

"Last time I checked, a person could hike around her own property any time she pleases." She brushed by him, the flannel of her checkered jacket rubbing his arm.

He moved to block the steps. "And it didn't occur to you that other people might worry?"

She gave a derisive snort—the verbal equivalent of giving him the finger—and looked amused at the thought. "I saw Amos at lunch and again later. He told me you'd been by."

Seth would have bought the nonchalance if he couldn't see the exhaustion in her face. He reined in his temper. "I'd like a few minutes of your time."

She nodded, and, waving for him to move out of the way, started up the stairs. Jack and Zack followed, looking as worn out as she did. When they reached the kitchen, they plopped down, their eyes following Rachel's progress to the chair. They switched their stare to him, and he felt as if their assessment fell short of ideal.

"What can I do for you, Sheriff?"

A blunt woman would expect a blunt response.

"You can explain why you never told me about your father."

The pain showed in her rigid spine, but she never missed a beat. "I don't see why my family history is any of your business."

He took a seat facing her, choosing his words with care. "The fact that your father was a serial killer might be relevant to my investigation."

Her bleak eyes met his. "How could it be? He's been dead for ten years."

"I don't know." He pulled a miniature recorder from his pocket and laid it in front of her on the table. "But we need to find out."

She eyed the machine as if it might bite her, then gave a reluctant nod. "I don't see how I can help."

"Just give me some background, and we'll start there." He turned on the recorder and gave both their names and the date. "Your father, Marcus Worth, was killed ten years ago, in prison?"

"Yes."

"By another inmate?"

"That's correct."

Seth cleared his throat. "He was serving time for multiple counts of murder when that occurred. How many victims?"

"Eleven." She huffed in a breath. "That they know of."

"And all eleven were young women killed by having their throats slit?"

She nodded.

"Can you respond out loud, please?"

"Yes."

"Your father committed these crimes without an

accomplice, as far as anyone knew?"

"Yes."

She chose to say as little as possible, but at least she was answering his questions. "Do you know of any connection between your father's crimes and the murder this department is currently investigating?"

A muted whimper escaped her. "I would have told you. You have to believe I wouldn't keep that to myself." Now her hands grasped her opposite elbows as if she could keep it together through brute strength.

Seth clicked off the recorder and let the silence settle them both. "I would never put you through this if I had any choice."

"I know." The words seeped out as if they were her last. She whisked away the single rebellious tear that trailed down her cheek.

He tried, and failed, to guess what her life had been like. A huge amount of research awaited him—he could spare her some pain by getting a lot of his information from old files and newspaper archives. "Can you think about it and let me know if there was anyone from back then who might be responsible for this death? I can't imagine why a stranger would want to involve you."

She nodded.

"I'll step up patrols, especially at night. You need to phone if anything, I mean a disturbance of any kind, happens. I'd rather get out of bed for a false alarm than take unnecessary chances. Do you understand?"

"Yes." She stood.

He pinned her with a look to make his point. "What were you looking for in the woods today?"

"Anything that didn't belong."

At least she didn't deny it. "I gather you saw

nothing out of the ordinary?"

"Everything looked normal as far as I could see."

He shuddered to think what might have been waiting in the woods. Trying to respect her independence would be a rough road for them until they found their way through this mess. "Don't go anywhere you don't have to, okay?"

"Unless you think the grocery store is hiding assorted criminals, I don't think you have much to worry about with me."

At least she had regained some of her sarcasm. With anyone else he might have put a supporting arm around his or her shoulders, but he knew she wouldn't welcome the gesture. "Okay. Fair enough." Seth stood, amused when the dogs clustered around Rachel. Maybe they weren't a total loss as guard dogs after all. He moved to the door, then turned for one last look when she didn't follow. "I'll get as much information about your history as I can from the records, but I might need you to fill in a few blanks."

She nodded.

He let himself out, afraid to see the havoc his visit had caused if he looked back.

Chapter Five

Rachel sat rooted to her chair for quite a while, letting her breath wheeze in and out. Her asthma seldom reared its ugly head anymore, but somehow always managed to show up in times of prolonged stress. The nightmare of these last few days refused to let her lungs return to normal. The empathy in Seth's face had almost been her undoing. It proved easier to suffer slaps and jeers, something she'd grown used to. *And what to do now? Just sit and wait?*

Jack and Zack padded to the cupboard, aiming beseeching looks in her direction. A glance at the clock made her realize she'd missed their regular dinnertime by an hour. "Sorry, guys," she murmured, reaching into the cabinet to scoop out two large helpings of the dry food mix and dumping it into their metal bowls beside the refrigerator.

Crunching sounds filled the air, and the familiarity of it calmed her. The facts simply weren't persuasive enough to indulge in full-blown hysteria, even if she possessed the energy to summon a bout. The killer hadn't offered any specific knowledge about her, other than the fact that she lived alone, hardly a secret. The notion that the sheriff might be jumping the gun settled her further.

She would just put it out of her head and keep her eyes open. All she wanted was peace. *Is that too much to ask?*

****

Seth sat staring at the computer long after he should have headed home. An always-thoughtful Rosie had dropped a sandwich and two cookies off at his desk before she left for the day. He took an occasional bite, tasting nothing, riveted by the information on Rachel's father.

Marcus Worth had been a college professor, of all things. Both universities and his community had bestowed many awards on him. Scores of photos showed a smiling, gray-haired man, very handsome, managing a humble smile as he accepted each plaque.

But behind the congenial façade, a twisted mind lurked. Sometimes brilliance tangos with insanity and creates a monster.

Rachel's mother received the dubious credit for turning him in. Common consensus concluded the authorities would have never caught him otherwise. Within days of his sentencing, the quiet, well-spoken woman committed suicide at a local hotel, an empty bottle of pills, some trinkets, and a note for her daughter her only bequest.

"Dark Mark," as the newspapers dubbed him, went to prison after the jury levied multiple counts of life upon him. He refused the insanity plea his lawyers urged him to take, quoting such a thing would sully his name. His casual recounting of the facts of each murder made the case more horrifying. According to the newspaper reports, when asked why he did it, he'd simply smiled and replied, "Because I enjoyed it, of course."

Seth cursed and rubbed his forehead. This case was

a lot to take in, all at once.

The eleven women had been similar in physical type. Each had blonde hair and a slender build. The list of his victims included four students, two nurses, three teachers, a sales clerk, and a hairdresser. The detectives never found a connection between them, one of the problems that bogged down the investigation.

What caused his wife to be suspicious?

Seth went back through the copious printouts, unearthing a screaming headline that read, "Guess who turned in Dark Mark?" According to that article, the wife, Renee, had been suspicious of his frequent absences from the home and had noted his rather cavalier reactions to the reports on the missing women, an attitude far different from the one he displayed in public. When he started to pay unusual attention to his own daughter, the woman ran right to the police, unwilling to take the chance she was wrong. What kind of unusual attention, he wondered, scared to know the answer.

The last thing the professor ever said to his wife apparently took place at the sentencing phase of the trial. "You're smarter than you look, dear," he'd remarked, to the obvious delight of the press who'd smeared it over newsprint everywhere. The thought of it sent chills up Seth's spine.

How does Rachel sleep at night? Maybe she didn't. Maybe she lay awake and waited for monsters to come.

It made a helluva way to live your life.

The darkening shadows caused him to glance at his watch, and Seth felt startled when it read eight thirty. He noticed the largely uneaten sandwich, now wilted and unappetizing. Real food would give him some energy. He could head home and throw something together. It might be time to give his eyes a rest and do more reading in the comfort of his own house.

But he felt guilty, piling all the printed information into his briefcase. No matter how hard he tried to contain it, some of this stuff was bound to come out. How would Rachel be able to stand the scrutiny?

****

Rachel lay on the floor of the den, a dog nestled on either side. Their gentle snores provided an odd, soothing music that kept her company. She'd been reading Twain to keep her mind off her troubles, but the dogs became pushy. They shoved under her arms to position themselves, and she put down the book to hug them. Rubbing a cheek against the softness of their coats provided the most elemental kind of comfort.

She doubted she'd be able to sleep. Images of her parents slipped through her thoughts, one welcome and the other dreaded.

Her mother's memory represented the good things—warm cookies and big, cuddly hugs. Her father, on the other hand, existed only as a caricature, past and present. He covered his natural responsibilities, like paying the mortgage and sitting with them at dinner, but she never felt at all connected to him. She'd always thought the fault for that lack fell to her.

In retrospect, perhaps that distance resulted in some kind of internal warning system. Because when he had indeed started paying attention to her, too much attention, little warning bells alerted her mother, like a discordant choir.

Rachel owed her mother her life. Because those bells had rung, she had stepped up the watch, never leaving them alone together. When his focus evolved into a kind of exuberant mania, her parent had put the torturous pieces together and snatched her out of harm's way.

Her mother acted as savior, but Rachel had been unable to return the favor, failing to recognize the anguish her mother could no longer bear. She often wondered if she had just begged her mom to stay home, would that intentional delay have thwarted her self-destruction. She would never know.

She sighed and buried her face in Jack's coat. That action earned her a sleepy lick on one cheek. The bastard who dumped these dogs gave her the only gift she'd received in years. They provided comfort that couldn't be bought at any store.

Rachel's thoughts swung to the sheriff. Seth seemed like a good man, but allowing herself to trust anyone didn't come naturally. By sheer force of will, she blocked out the almost ferocious guilty pleasure she experienced at the sight of that big, strong body wrapped in khakis and cotton. She'd watched every woman in town drool after him as he walked the streets, even the old bats. And, who knows, maybe that chemical reaction would result in some enjoyable dreams instead of the haunting kind that usually plagued her.

She knew it wouldn't, but sometimes, hope kept her breathing.

She thought about going to bed and then decided to stay put. Moving would probably just wake up all three of them and make the dogs restless. She snuggled in and closed her eyes.

****

First thing in the morning, Seth finally received the information on the third missing person and knew right away he had a match. The ears and chin of his victim gave it away, but he sent the information, including dental charts, down to Doc so he could make it official.

He felt a surge of pity for the parents of Candy Parks. She had only been missing a week, so they likely still held out hope of a happy ending. Notifying next of kin was, without a doubt, the ugliest part of his job.

Seth scanned the information on the sheet. A second-year nursing student, Candy disappeared after leaving her apartment to pick up some groceries. It was one of those unsettling cases where no clues could be found. A patrolman had discovered her car days later near a dump, wiped down and vacuumed. No one remembered seeing her at the store. Local police were stymied, and so was Seth.

He needed a small crack in the case, anything he could use to figure out the future plans of this freak. That note taunted him—killers seldom made promises they didn't keep.

Seth spent the morning reviewing all his notes, interrupted around noon by the expected confirmation from Doc. He called the department handling the disappearance of Candy Parks and experienced rather pathetic relief when they confirmed they would take care of the notification themselves.

Life in the country softened everyone, including him.

He had requested crime scene photos from the "Dark Mark" cases and ended up spending a long half hour on the phone, explaining why he wanted them. The detective who reluctantly agreed to send that part of the file treated him like some half-wit until Seth offered a few names he could contact to prove his credentials. After the officer checked out the information, cooperation was forthcoming. He was told the photo file would be sent by that afternoon.

When he returned from lunch, he found the expected photographs on his desk, printed out courtesy of Rosie. Taking a seat, he settled back and ripped open the envelope. They spilled onto his desk, the grisly kind that made even seasoned detectives wince. Eleven women, whose hopes and dreams for the future culminated in tragedy.

He hoped to find something, anything, that would prove his hunch false, some clear indication that no connection existed between this case and his own. He searched through the pile for the first victim.

And felt his heart sink. He took a deep breath, forcing himself to look past the superficial resemblance of the blonde hair. But even after a few minutes of painful perusal, the similarities still stared up at him—a pert, upturned nose, thin lips, and the more pathetic identical injuries, the gaping slashes that bisected each woman's throat.

He felt a surge of pity for this long-dead woman and then an almost equal surge for himself. Because Seth knew, without a doubt, that with just a strong hunch and a few inexperienced men, he had no hope of catching this killer before he struck again.

Chapter Six

Rachel heard the cellphone ringing as she returned from her evening walk. She didn't hurry to answer, not really caring if she caught it in time. As she pulled off her jacket, the ringing stopped. The message simply asked that she call Seth.

She took her time, feeding the dogs and climbing into soft cotton pajamas. Finally, scooching back in the big easy chair, she called the second number scrawled on the card. Not bothering with pleasantries, she said, "You were looking for me?" as soon as he answered the phone.

He met her, tit for tat. "Did the authorities ever figure out why your father chose to kill only blondes?"

She huffed out the answer. "No."

"In the newspaper photographs your mother was a brunette. Did she ever dye her hair?"

She shut her eyes against Renee's conjured image. "She was always a brunette. They made a big point of asking her that, as if she could have been responsible for whatever trigger set him off." She couldn't stop the bitter bite in her enunciated words.

"I'm sorry."

She knew he meant it. Reining herself in, she said, "It's hardly your fault. I know that." After a few seconds of silence, she added, "Have you found out our victim's identity?"

"Yes. Another department notified next of kin this afternoon." He cleared his throat. "She was a nursing student."

The implication set in. "And one of my father's victims was a nurse, right?"

"Yes."

"It's just a coincidence." The words rushed out of her as if saying them fast enough might make it true.

"It might be."

"But you don't think so."

He sighed, and the sound seemed to groan through the phone. "I compared the photos of both women. There are strong similarities."

The words battered her with memories and dark fears too numerous to name.

"Rachel."

She regained her focus. "I'm sorry."

"Are you okay?"

"I guess so."

Seth apologized. "I don't get any pleasure from putting you through this."

"I understand your position. Call me again if I can help." Switching off the phone, she placed it on the table and, slumping back, shut her eyes.

Her thoughts circled round and round until the strain created a headache that pounded across her forehead. She forced herself into the kitchen for at least some cheese and crackers, hoping food would help. A half hour later, the pain only intensified. In a fit of desperation, she went to sit on the front steps, hoping the swirl of cold air might lesson the pain. The dogs followed her, looking surprised, then thumping down on the porch beside her.

She counted slowly in her mind, breathing in and out, practicing the relaxation exercises she'd done for years. After twenty minutes, the pain started to ease and she almost cried in relief. She laid a hand on Jack's back and he leaped to his feet.

"It's okay, Jack," she whispered, then realized he didn't respond. Instead, the hair stood up on his ruff and he growled, his head lifting as his brother jumped up to mimic him.

Rachel eased to her feet. The dark swallowed everything but the steps and a small strip of driveway. She scanned around her, out of habit. "Let's go inside," she murmured, hoping her voice would calm them.

They exploded into noise, barks and howls, vibrating with undeniable ferocity.

She reached for the door, calling them, when she heard something pierce the air around her head. Her subconscious recognized the whine of a bullet before she did and she plunged through the opening as soon as she could wrestle the handle, screaming for the dogs. She fell on the tiled floor, then crawled the rest of the way inside, sobbing their names until they bounded through after her.

Kicking the door shut, Rachel stretched one arm up to lock the dead bolt. Too frightened to reach for the gun in the closet, she kept down, away from the window. In the dim background, she heard the phone ringing. Fear kept her pinned to the floor, holding the dogs even as they bristled and snarled. She kept repeating, "We're okay, we're okay," not sure if even she believed it. Heaving air into her lungs, she wondered if a simple lock and two loyal dogs were enough to keep the killer out.

****

Seth gunned the car around the corner, scattering gravel everywhere. *Shots fired, by God, and Rachel isn't answering her phone.* Amos had been beside himself when he called, almost incoherent, forcing Seth to threaten him into staying put until he could investigate.

His vehicle roared up the long hill to the front of the house, sliding to a halt beside the steps. Sitting for a moment, Seth let his high beams play over the nearby lawn. Exiting slowly, he stayed flat against the bumper, his gun at the ready. He swept the powerful flashlight in a big circle, illuminating the surrounding field. *Nothing.*

Seth could hear the dogs baying inside the house. Good for you, he thought. *Did you scare him away?* He inched up the stairs one step at a time, keeping his back to the house. "Rachel? It's Seth."

The door opened as if by magic, and he could see she'd stepped back, gripping the struggling dogs by their collars. He moved inside, closing the door behind him. Raising one hand to stop her questions, his other went to the radio at the collar of his jacket. "This is Seth. Rachel is inside, and she's fine. Let me talk to her, and I'll get back to you. And call Amos so he knows she's all right." He lowered his hand to calm the dogs. "It's okay, guys." They seemed to take his word for it and stopped struggling. Rachel released them and they stood like sentinels between them, still quivering.

"What happened?" He noticed her pale skin and motioned for her to sit down. "Amos called. They heard a gunshot, maybe two, and the dogs making a fuss."

She nodded, little more than a jerk of the head.

"Where were you when this happened?"

"On the front porch, at the top of the steps." Breath wheezed out of her, and he stepped to her side, only to have her wave him back. "I'm okay. It's just my asthma."

"Did you see anything?"

"No." She sat a little straighter to help push the words out. "The dogs started to growl and carry on, so I stood up to go in, then I heard that whistling sound. I think there might have been a second shot as I dove into the kitchen."

"Good reflexes." He caught the glimmer of a smile. "Did the dogs follow you in?"

"Yes. They didn't want to, but they did." Her breath heaved again, and she took a puff from an inhaler she dug out of her pocket.

"You gestured toward the east. Is that the direction the shots came from?"

She nodded. "Yes, east to west. It would have hit me in the ear, side to side, not head on."

"Okay. I want you to lock up behind me. Wayne is on his way, and we're going to have a look around."

Three minutes later, Wayne pulled up in his cruiser, lights rolling but no siren, thank goodness. Seth could already imagine all the excitement this would cause in the morning, but at the moment there were more pressing needs.

Wayne hopped out, his face pale in the moonlight. "Did you see anyone?"

"Nothing. I need you to sit here in your car and see that nobody makes an approach while I take a look around. I'll call you on the radio when I'm ready to return to the house. You see anybody except me nearby, hit the siren." Recognizing the disappointment on the young man's face, he continued. "I'm sure he's long gone, but we can't take any chances with Rachel, can we?"

"No, sir." Wayne lowered himself back inside. As Seth watched, his deputy laid his pistol on his lap.

Seth gave him a nod of approval before heading off into the night.

Chapter Seven

Rachel paced back and forth across the den, peeking out through a tiny crack in the curtain every few minutes. *Seth has totally lost his mind, wandering out there in the dark with a maniac on the loose. He could be killed.* The thought made every muscle in her body tense.

There must be some tiny piece of womanhood still alive in her. That fragment had been damned glad to see him roaring up the drive. She'd had to stem the wanton impulse to throw herself into those muscled arms.

Isn't that enough to turn a dog from his dinner.

For a few minutes Rachel watched young Wayne acting as sentry. Too young for this job, she thought. Hunting down a killer took experience, and once in a while, just dumb luck. On the other hand, sometimes it just took a mother driven to a horrendous task. She pushed the thought away.

The dogs finally settled, only to leap to their feet when Seth knocked almost an hour after he'd left. She eased it open and read the frustration on his face. "Nothing?"

Seth shook his head. "Can I come in?"

Realizing she'd been blocking his way, she stepped back.

He shut the door behind him. "I didn't really expect to find anything, but I had to check. We might have more luck in the morning." He stared down at her. "I'd like to stay here tonight."

"You…what did you say?"

Her confusion made him smile. "I could stay out in my car, but I was hoping you might lend me your easy chair for the rest of the night."

Well, that presented a different picture than had first leapt to mind. "I appreciate your concern, but it's really not necessary." Rachel ignored the needy part of her that clamored for his company. "I'm sure whoever it is, is long gone."

Sighing, he crossed his arms. "I just can't take the chance."

"Oh, for goodness sake." She swallowed relief. "If you get your jollies by sitting in my recliner waiting to be a hero, go ahead." To gain a minute, she went to the bedroom closet and hauled out a blanket and pillow. Having Seth in the house meant no sleep for her, but she probably wouldn't have slept anyway. Rachel stomped back into the den. The dogs nosed around the chair until she growled at them to sit down.

It wasn't until then that Rachel realized she wore only pajamas. Dropping the bedclothes in the chair, she flew back into the bedroom, grabbing for the old flannel robe on the bedpost. Seth's chuckle sounded from the den, and she gritted her teeth. *Who invited him, anyway.* Rachel re-entered the room, snugging the belt around her waist. "What else do you need?"

"Not a thing." He smiled. "You'll find I'm pretty easy to have around."

"I'm sure dozens have thought so," she responded and cringed at the sheer bitchiness of her reply. To make amends, she fetched a glass of water from the kitchen and held it out. “Want some?”

He nodded his thanks when she handed it to him and took a swig.

She filled one for herself. “Did you send Wayne home?”

“Yes.” He smiled. “I think he wanted to bite a bigger piece of trouble than the nip he caught tonight.”

“It’ll end up being some fool just getting a start on the hunting season,” she offered, trying to inject some belief into her tone.

His grin faded. “We might just have to call that the best-case scenario for now.”

After his comment, even the sip of water seemed stale, and she bid him goodnight, adding there was food in the refrigerator if he felt hungry.

Hours later, Rachel stared at the early morning light trickling onto the ceiling. She’d managed to get about four hours sleep in one stretch, a damn record in recent years. Right now, she could barely convince herself to move, registering the sounds of Seth’s footsteps as the unmistakable aroma of fresh-brewed coffee filtered into her room. Even the dogs had deserted their treasured spot beside the bed for his company.

What would it be like to attract everyone instead of repel them? Rachel had been a pariah for so long she couldn’t imagine. Shaking away the thought, she crawled out of bed, stretching cramped limbs, and reached into the closet. Finding an outfit required no effort. Jeans and a fresh shirt would be on the left side of the closet. At the end of the day, her clothes went into the laundry basket. Once a week, she washed and dried her unimaginative wardrobe and organized the system for the following week. A bureau by the window held neat rows of white athletic socks, cotton underpants and bras, an even dozen of each. She ordered new ones online from Boring.com.

Rachel dressed in her chosen uniform and brushed long hair into the tail that kept it off her face. Taking a deep breath, she opened the door. The reality of Seth standing there, sock-footed in her kitchen, stopped her cold. “Good morning,” she managed.

“Morning,” he answered. He held up one hand, displaying a half-eaten apple. “I helped myself. Hope it’s okay.”

Nodding, she forced herself to move forward. “There’s cereal, too, if you like.”

“This will be enough for now. I’m going to try and figure out where our visitor fired from last night. If we can, we might be able to find a spent shell.”

Rachel felt his gaze on her as she laced battered boots and pulled on a jacket. He followed suit. The dogs circled their legs until the door opened, then they bounded ahead. The scary night had changed to a gleaming day, the sun so bright it made a joke of bad guys.

Seth paused for a minute at the top of the steps on the porch. Turning his face to the sun, he asked, “Was this about where you were when you heard the shots?”

“A little more to the left.” A shiver caught her by surprise. He changed his position, and she realized he was trying to figure out the angle of the shot. After he inspected the front of the house, she said, “He shot right to left.”

“I know. I’m just double-checking you got the angle right.”

She began to accompany him down the steps when he moved.

"No. Stay right there for me." Seth walked a long way off, stopping just before he disappeared into the trees on the upper side and raising his arms, as if he cradled a rifle. After a few minutes, he returned. "Let's take a walk the other way. If we can find a spent casing, that at least would give us something to work with. It's a little strange the shooter would choose to aim at your profile, rather than head on."

They strolled slowly, the dogs trotting in front of them until they reached the trees on the opposite side of the porch. Every now and then, Seth would stop, peer back at the house, and alter his direction a little bit. Rachel observed him scanning up and down the trunks of the trees and mimicked his action, wondering what the chances were they would uncover something.

After an hour, she started to twitch with boredom.

"There you are, you little bugger."

She moved to stand beside Seth, peering along the level of his pointed finger. The bullet was located much higher than she had been looking, wedged into the bark of a large tree. Tiny splinters surrounded the entry. "Are you going to pull it out?"

"In a minute." He shifted to dig in his pockets and came up with a set of keys. "I need you to go into my trunk and bring out the zippered bag I keep there." He paused, frowning. "I don't suppose you have a small handsaw, do you?"

She nodded.

"Can you bring that, too? I don't want to risk damaging the bullet when I remove it."

Rachel jogged back along the route they had taken.

She opened the car trunk and wasn't surprised to find it almost military neat. Digging around the first aid kit and his rifle in its case, she found the blue nylon tote bag. With it in one hand, she slammed the trunk and jogged around to the side of the house, lifting her little saw from a hook under the porch. On returning to the woods, she found the dogs sitting at Seth's feet and called them away.

"They're not bothering me." He retrieved the bag and the saw from her and set them on the ground. The first things he withdrew were a pair of gloves and a small, zippered bag he poked into his shirt pocket. Then came the camera to take the necessary pictures. Picking up the saw, he cut a neat square around the bullet, not very deep, then stopped and pulled on the gloves. A few hard squeezes on either side and the bullet popped out into his hand. "Bingo." He transferred it to the bag. He looked through the plastic. "It's a .243. Pretty common rifle ammunition. We'll see what else the lab can tell us." Pulling a bright orange strip from the bag, he tied it around the tree. "I'll get Wayne up here to finish and see what else he can find. They'll be waiting for me at the station."

They traipsed back toward the house. Seth turned and smiled. "I can hear questions buzzing around in your mind, but you're keeping them to yourself."

"What can a bullet tell you?"

Seth shrugged. "The grooves can help us identify the rifle. Maybe we get lucky and his weapon is a rare one only a few people own." He met her gaze. "More realistically, it gives us a tiny start on a profile of this guy."

They arrived at the side of the car, and she reached

to take the saw from him. “Better than nothing, I guess.”

“We have to start somewhere.” Nodding, he slid onto the front seat, stopping to pat the dogs who had appeared at the open door. “I’ll check in with you later.”

And as he drove away, she knew he would do exactly as he promised.

Chapter Eight

The next day, Rachel spent the afternoon looking up old newspaper articles in a town thirty minutes away where no one knew her. She kept no possessions from her old life at the house, nothing except her mother's ring, a raggedy Bible, and a box of trinkets.

The screaming headlines signaling the devastating end of her childhood filled the front pages for months after her father's arrest. One said, "The Legacy of Dark Mark" and had a photo of Rachel being hustled off by her mother, wrapped up in a shapeless coat. After these incidents with the press, her mother would sob for hours, fighting to stifle it and losing the battle.

Rachel couldn't be sure exactly when her mother had given up. It wasn't a sudden decision, she thought, but a process, like an abscess that grows too inflamed to heal. After her mother had abandoned hope, Rachel thought about following her, just closing her eyes and being carried, hopefully, into miraculous peace. Or would she end up in hell, she wondered, cursed with the blood of evil incarnate? That fear kept her alive, the fear of flames licking the soles of her feet as she ran.

He was an anomaly, her father. Serial killers were often underachievers, people who blamed the world for their own incompetence or lack of motivation. Her father was one of those celebrated few who had always basked in the limelight of their own imagined genius and found the rest of the world wanting.

As a young child, she'd thought him so handsome with his premature silver hair and those piercing gray eyes. Only when she grew older did she recognize the emptiness that lived there in the mirrors to his soul.

Picture after picture of him sprang to light on the microfilm, with a wide smile for the camera as he was led to and from the courtroom. During the trial, he even managed to woo a pathetic following who refused to believe he could be guilty. "Well, I am, of course," he assured them, enjoying the groans and tears that would inevitably follow.

Rachel came here to try and find answers, not to wallow in the sludge of his life. But she didn't know what to look for—maybe look under "A" for answers to this bizarre riddle. *Who killed that poor girl?*

Seth thought the killer was a copycat. What kind of person followed a pattern of horror? Had someone watched her father from the throngs of people who followed the case, ready to pay homage to him? But why wait so long? Her father had been dead for years.

She stared at the legal pad and pen she'd brought with her, not knowing where to begin. It was up to her to figure it out. Hours later, the librarian tapped her on the shoulder, making her jump, and said the library would be closing in a few minutes. The poor woman's eyes bugged out when she saw the images on the screen, and she scurried off with one horrified backwards glance. Rachel gathered up her barely-touched notepad and left, feeling the woman's hot stare on her back.

Rachel drove home, on autopilot, to find both Seth and Amos on her steps, the dogs at their feet. Ignoring

Seth's glare, she leaned down to pat them.

"Where have you been?"

She arched an eyebrow as she straightened. "I've been conducting my life, like any citizen is free to do in this country."

Amos looked disappointed in her. "We were worried, Rachel. It's not like you to be gone so long."

"I can take care of myself." They made her feel like a wayward child. "Did you think I'd run away?"

Amos glanced back and forth between the two of them and sighed. "Guess I'll leave you two to work it out between you. I've got cattle to feed." He started walking toward his tractor, parked a dozen feet from where they stood.

Rachel squirmed. "Amos," she called after a moment.

He turned toward her, his expression sober.

"I'm sorry I worried you."

He nodded, then climbed up on the tractor and started it. Powering up the throttle, he turned, driving back over the hill.

Ignoring Seth, she climbed up the steps, then, cursing, turned and came back down. "I forgot. The dogs need a walk."

"I already took them."

Somehow, the arrogance of assuming he could made her twitch. "They're not your dogs."

His face flushed, and a vein in his temple throbbed. "You weren't here when I arrived at five. They were circling around, looking pathetic. I thought it would take their minds, and mine, from focusing on the fact you'd run off."

"I didn't run off. I—"

"You what, Rachel?"

And just like that, it slipped out. "I was trying to figure out who is responsible for all this."

"All what?" He said the words with emphasis, teeth clamped together. "I know you're not trying to solve this case on your own, Rachel, because that would be irresponsible, wouldn't it? It might put you right in a killer's path."

She started to stalk by him, her heart beating a terrible tattoo, but he grabbed her arm.

"I've already been in a killer's path," she yelled. "Do you think I want to be there again?" Whirling away, she ran up the steps, slamming the door before the bewildered dogs could follow.

Inside, Rachel leaned into the doorway to the living room, trying to hold back tears. She dimly registered the quiet opening and closing of the door, accompanied by the subdued steps of both dogs and man. A tentative hand landed on her shoulder. The touch almost made her gasp. She shut her eyes. *It would be so much safer for me if he would just leave.* It was an odd thought, born of desperation. She should treasure Seth, the only one who stood between her and an obsessed maniac.

"Where were you?" His question came in a different tone this time, and when she turned, she read compassion in his expression.

"At the library in Alton." She turned to face him. "I thought if I looked at all of the newspaper articles, something might jump out at me."

He nodded. "That couldn't have been easy."

His understanding was almost more than she could bear. "It didn't help. It's all a jumble."

"Rachel, of course it's a jumble. You're not in law

enforcement. Even trained professionals strain to make sense of these things." He gestured toward the chairs. "Let's sit for a minute. Okay?"

She sat at a diagonal position from him so she wouldn't have to stare right into those intuitive eyes.

"I sent the bullet to ballistics this morning, along with a couple of casings we found on the other side of the hill. Maybe they can tell us something."

"How long will it take?"

"If we're lucky, maybe a week. I'm calling in some favors."

She breathed in and let the air trickle out again. "I thought of one thing that might be considered good news. My father waited for three months between his first two victims so a copycat will wait a similar length of time. Right?"

He stared at her.

She knew that look by now. It was his "I hate being the bearer of bad news' look.

Seth cleared his throat. "Copycats don't always follow the original script. Sometimes they just lose control. Other times, they think they can improve on the first crime, or in this case, crimes."

"Terrific."

He worried about Rachel taking this so personally, as if something she had done triggered this mess. "We don't know anything for sure, at this point. Maybe we'll get lucky."

She laughed, but the sound had nothing to do with humor. "I'm not too familiar with luck."

"I can't imagine how you feel, but I can sympathize." He stood, stepping away from the table. "We'll continue to do drive-bys as frequently as we can. Let us know if you see anything out of the ordinary, even if it seems unimportant. Promise me?"

She nodded and rose to see him out of the door. "Goodnight."

" 'Night, Rachel."

She watched as he drove slowly down the drive, scanning the tree line on both sides.

****

Rosie came through the office door, closing it behind her, never a good sign. Seth looked up from his paperwork. "What's up?"

His assistant grimaced. "Brady."

Seth sighed. "What's he done now?"

"Apparently, he was pissed off Wayne got assigned to Rachel's case and not him, so he spilled the beans about the second note."

Seth swore. "Who did he tell?"

"He told a couple guys down at Smiley's while they were havin' a few beers. Who knows who they told."

Seth tried to rein in his temper. "Where is he?"

"Talking to Mr. Baker about those kids who stole smokes from his store."

"Tell him to come and see me when he's done."

"Okay, Seth. Will do." She left, closing the door behind her.

What the hell is his problem? And he wonders why I never let him deal with the more challenging cases? He'll be lucky he still has a job. Seth tried to ignore the throbbing in his head and reached into his desk drawer for aspirin, only to find the bottle empty. Leaning out, he asked Rosie for a few tablets, which she supplied with a sympathetic look.

The rest of the day proved equally frustrating, with no further light shed on his biggest issue. The humdrum pursuit of cigarette thieves and lost pets filled the hours until Brady finally showed up, without much of an explanation of why it had taken him so long to accomplish such an easy task.

The plodding day didn't leave Seth in a good mood. "Sit," he said, gesturing to the chair opposite his.

Brady did as he was told, taking his time.

"What don't you understand about keeping information about our cases to yourself?"

Brady tipped his hat up, with a smirk. "Not sure what you're talkin' about, boss."

"You told your buddies at the bar about the letter we found at Rachel's."

He shrugged. "I don't recall sayin' much, but it might have come up. Who told you?"

"You were overheard by more than one person, and I think you're missing the point. It's essential any information on this murder stays between these four walls."

Brady had the poor sense to chuckle. "Come on, Seth, get a grip. That nutty bitch on the hill knows stuff, and Abe knows stuff and who knows who else. You can't keep this crap private in a small town."

Seth wanted to punch this idiot in the face but reined in the impulse. "No, thanks to you we can't keep it private. From now on, you don't have access to any notes on this case. If I see you poking your nose in, you're fired."

"Listen, big shot, I've got friends—"

Seth stood up. "I don't give a damn about your friends. One more violation and you're out. You're dismissed."

Cursing, Brady stood, then stomped out, slamming the office door in childish defiance. After a moment, Seth heard the front door slam as well.

It was past time to go home. He peered out and saw Rosie putting on her coat. The night dispatcher waited to one side, ready to take her desk. "You heading out, boss?"

"Yup. Tell Wayne to call me if he needs anything."

****

Carson Gale sat in a hotel room a few towns over, paging through the book of his favorite clippings. His friend and mentor, Marcus Worth, stared out of every page. The prison fight had been a most unfair end to a brilliant life.

People had been awed by Marcus but hadn't stood by him through his hardships, not like Carson had. Only he had understood Marcus had been put on earth to do exactly what he did, share his philosophies with the world and then get everything that was his rightful due.

No, the women ruined everything. They always did. They wanted both the attention of being seen on Dark Mark's arm and then to control him as well. *The greedy bitches.* That sniveling little wife of his, who thought she would have the brains to put the clues together. *Look where it landed her*. Just another slut on a slab as Mark used to say.

And the daughter, what a joke. She changes her name and moves a few times to try and avoid detection. It had been child's play to find her, living like the town freak with only a few mutts for company. Watching her dive through the door had made him laugh out loud the other night, before he disappeared over the hill to avoid the sheriff coming from the other direction. Did she really think he meant to kill her last night? If he had, she'd be in the morgue instead of Blondie, number one.

He had to decide what was next on the agenda. Terrorize Rachel or give her another present to brighten her day.

Chapter Nine

Wayne waited by his office door when Seth showed up the next morning. Seth glance at his watch. “You’re an hour early, Wayne. What’s up?” He waved him inside.

The deputy stood in front of the desk as Seth took his seat. “I did the morning check by Rachel’s place this morning.”

“See anything?”

He nodded, looking excited. “I went for a walk on the west side since I was early for work.”

“You’re lucky she didn’t shoot you,” Seth commented.

The other man shook his head. “I called to tell her what I was planning. She gave me permission. Anyway, I think I found a looking post.”

“What exactly did you find, Wayne?”

He grinned. “A little pile of candy wrappers and two cans.”

“Could just be kids.”

“The line of sight is perfect for Rachel’s front porch.”

That caught Seth’s attention. “Well, I guess we know where we’re headed next. Okay to start early?”

“Yes, sir.”

The boy looked as pleased as punch, and Seth didn’t blame him. He grabbed the keys and beckoned the younger man to follow.

****

Seth called Rachel and told her they were headed to the pasture for yet another look around. She knew the deputy had found something earlier as she saw him bound back to the car with youthful enthusiasm. At least it couldn't be another body. He wouldn't have had a smile on his face if that was the case.

She had already been on her walk and now the dogs lay snoozing at her feet while she went through the monthly statements on her business income. She worked for about another thirty minutes before she heard the anticipated knock on the door. Without much choice, she went to answer it.

"Good morning, Rachel." Seth stood there, hat in one hand, sunglasses in the other. "Has everything been quiet?"

She nodded. "So far, anyway. What did the kid find?"

He smiled. "The 'kid' is a twenty-four-year-old deputy."

"He looks sixteen."

"True. I guess he'll be thankful for his appearance later on."

She waited for the reason for his visit.

"Wayne found the sniper's nest."

"How can you be sure?"

"There's food wrappers and a few soda cans and flattened grass where he made himself comfortable."

"That's too easy. It could just be kids."

"Except the sight line reaches straight to your porch."

"Oh, I see." She did see, but she didn't have to like

it.

He smiled as the dogs wandered out from the open door, yawning. He leaned down to pat them. "I have two night vision cameras, leftovers from my old days in New York. Wondered if you mind if I put them in the trees on the off chance he comes back to the same location?"

She shrugged. "Sure. As long as it's you or Wayne who's going to be checking on them and not that idiot Brady Doss."

"Fair enough." He put his hat and glasses back on. "Have a good day, Rachel."

"Okay." She watched him open the door and remembered to add, "You, too."

The day passed without issue, her only excitement being a trip to the grocery. As usual, the clerks whispered about her as she exited, something she barely noticed anymore. For a real treat, she made a juicy, medium rare steak for the three of them, leaving most of it to the dogs. She had a little more fun with the baked potato, adding extra butter and cheese, feeling the need for comfort food.

Shortly afterwards, she sat on the porch with the dogs, watching Seth walking back and forth to his car as he installed the cameras. The sun was starting to set, and she wondered why he had left it so late. He drove up to the porch afterwards as she munched on a cookie from the bag she had brought to the porch with her. "Sorry I'm so late."

"I was wondering whether you would run out of daylight."

He shook his head. "The Gardeners had another screaming fight, right in the middle of Main Street. By the time I arrived, they each had a sibling lined up, egging them on." He smiled. "Same old, same old. It's the third time this year."

"Even I know about them. They should do you a favor and get divorced."

"Promise you, by tomorrow, they'll be pledging undying love for each other." He laughed. "Happens every time, like clockwork."

She held out the bag of cookies, offering him one. The surprise on his face spoke volumes. "I figured you probably missed dinner," she said, embarrassed she'd offered.

"Can I have a couple?"

She nodded, and he dug in, pulling two out and biting into the first one. "I heard the parents of the poor girl have been notified."

He took a minute to chew and swallow. "Yeah. I'm glad the locals had to take care of it. It's the worst part of my job."

"What's the best part?"

Seth looked thoughtful as he wiped a crumb from the corner of his lips. "Just helping people out, I guess. It's a lot of little things. That's what I missed when I was in New York." He leaned against the rail. "How about you? Do you like it enough to stay?"

His question caught her off guard. "I like it a lot, but I guess it depends on how this mess turns out."

"You can't run forever, Rachel."

She felt torn between lashing out and asking for a hug, which astonished her. She leaned down and picked up the bag of cookies and her glass. "It's the only thing I'm good at," she answered, and opening the door, slipped inside.

****

At home later that evening, Seth kept hearing Rachel's parting words repeat in his memory. Rosie was right, as usual. Proud, prickly Rachel Mann might be the loneliest person he'd ever met. He couldn't imagine going through such tragedy at any age, much less seventeen. The additional information he'd dug up said she had lived less than a year in foster care until the age of consent and then simply disappeared off the radar. She couldn't make the name change disappear from legal records, but she'd done the best she could while still living a somewhat normal life.

Just for a minute, there on the porch, he'd felt like giving her a hug to console her. The impulse had surprised him. He felt certain it would have shocked the hell out of her. She wasn't his type. At least thus far, he had looked for uncomplicated, happy women. There had never been any temptation to secure a permanent arrangement. His parents had passed on, too early, and the folks in town were the closest thing he had to family. He and Rachel had that much in common, at least.

Seth popped open a can of beer and took the plate full of chips and roast beef sandwich he'd prepared to his recliner. Switching on the news depressed him, so he changed to a sitcom which entertained him just long enough to finish his meal. A few minutes before ten p.m., he nodded off.

In the morning, he felt refreshed, although he'd spent all night in the recliner again, which gave him a crick in his neck the shower had to pound out. He pulled on fresh pants, noting it was laundry time, his least favorite job. Chewing down a bowl of cereal gave him time to text Wayne to let him know he would check the cameras on his way to work.

He parked in the lower pasture, took out his tool kit, and climbed the hill, listening for any movement. There was nothing but the birds chirping and Amos's cattle mooing in the distance. The earthy smell of the last cutting of hay filled his nostrils. He reached the spot where he'd left the cameras.

They were gone. He saw the wires dangling and swore a blue string of words, glad no one was listening. Then he caught sight of the open note, anchored once again by a rock. *Having fun, Sheriff? I sure am.* There were two more words on the bottom. *Tick Tock.*

Seth unzipped the tool kit, took the necessary pictures, and slipped the note into a bag. He was inspecting the grass, muttering to himself, when he heard approaching footsteps. His hand went to the gun on his hip, before a voice called, "It's me." Rachel appeared through the trees, no dogs in sight.

"Stay there."

She stopped. "What did you find?"

He heard the quiver in her voice she couldn't smother. "It's what I didn't find. The cameras are gone, and he left another note."

She swore.

"That's what I said." He finished and started down the hill toward her. "I thought you were going to keep the dogs with you."

"They're on a stay at the bottom of the hill."

"Let's go join them." They walked together down the slope. When they cleared the trees, he could see both dogs lying at the bottom of the hill, squirming, but in place, their tails wagging a welcome.

Rachel said, “Free.” They hopped to their feet and made a beeline for Seth, heads tilted up for a welcoming hand. When he and Rachel reached the car, he tucked the evidence away and then stretched down to pat them. They pushed at each other, vying for attention. “They certainly like you,” Rachel said.

“Don’t be so surprised,” he joked. “Animals and old ladies always love me. It’s everyone else who isn’t sure.”

She looked back up the slope. “What are you going to do now?”

He shrugged. “I’m spending as much time as I can going over the old files. I think there has to be a clue somewhere, assuming it’s a copycat.”

“We won’t know much more until someone else dies.”

I wish she was wrong. “If that happens, I’ll likely have to call in the FBI. We just don’t have the resources to handle a bigger investigation.”

“You don’t need them.” Her tone, suddenly harsh, matched her accusing eyes.

He sighed. “I understand how you feel….”

“You couldn’t possibly understand how I feel.” She turned and began to stalk away, the dogs ambling behind.

“Rachel.”

She picked up speed, heading for the house, and he recognized the need to let her escape.

Well, isn’t this day starting off with a bang. Seth opened the car door and slid in, slamming the door. The sound had the dogs turning to look back, then they hurried to catch up to Rachel. Every time he made some progress with her, they suffered a setback. How welcome would his visits be now?

Later in the day, he combed through the case notes, his eyes blurry with fatigue. He'd already snapped at Rosie and had to apologize, treating her to lunch from their favorite haunt, including a monster size piece of red velvet cake, her favorite. At least everything else proved quite routine.

He couldn't kick the feeling of dread, deep in his gut. A call from the lab told him, although they had just started on the wrappers and cans he'd sent them, so far, the garbage was "suspiciously clean" and they weren't optimistic.

Great.

He'd asked for advice from an old friend from homicide who assured him he was doing everything possible, but he kept up a fruitless search for an ultimate clue. It simply didn't exist. Not yet, at least.

The undeniable truth was the next clue might have to come via another helpless victim's body.

****

Victim number two smiled at Carson from her table across the coffee shop. He responded by toasting her with his cup and then going back to his newspaper. It wouldn't do to acknowledge her in a more visceral way, although it was unlikely the harried baristas and impatient customers would notice. They were too busy paying eight dollars for what was essentially a coffee milkshake.

His drink represented a premature celebration of sorts. The student he'd toasted stopped here every morning to study, and he happened to be here at the same time. When he stopped to chat with her twenty minutes from now, he would seem like just another familiar face, wouldn't he?

Glancing at his watch, he felt his adrenaline begin to rev. *Showtime.* He folded the newspaper and stood, grabbing his briefcase and pushing the chair to the table. Watching the girl in the reflection of the glass, he saw her take note of his exit. She looked at her own watch.

Perfect. He loved a punctual sacrifice. A lot of people used the alley to access the university campus. For him, the length of the shortcut allowed two clear opportunities to strike. It always paid to have a fallback plan.

He stood in the shade of a spreading oak, using a small hand mirror to look over his shoulder. When she turned the corner and started down the alley, her relaxed gait gave him plenty of time to maneuver the sap into his right hand. As she started toward the trees, he dropped his fake cellphone to the ground, along with some files that spilled out of his hand. With a curse, he set down the briefcase with his left hand. As he bent over, he turned slightly so she could see his face.

"Do you need some help?"

He smiled. "That would be lovely."

Chapter Ten

Rachel snapped at Jack for getting under her feet, and he gave her a wounded look and went to lie in the corner, away from her.

Great. Now even the dogs will be running away from me.

She blamed the FBI, in part, for her mother's death. Their constant hounding had forced her into a tortured endgame. First, she had to help them catch her husband, then she had to suffer the implication she, herself, might have been involved. It proved to be too much of a burden for a woman who had already suffered so much heartbreak.

Rachel had learned to trust Seth, at least a little, but the feds were another story. Who could hate her enough to make her go through this again? She didn't know anyone well enough to instill this much emotion.

She couldn't figure out how to help Seth. Was she just supposed to wait this out? If so, a padded room might be her destiny.

Making up her mind, she stood, calling the dogs. They jumped up, looking confused, as well they should. A full two hours before their normal evening walk made a huge change in their schedule, but what else could she do except keep up the patrol. Wearing her gun on her walks had become habit. She kept it strapped in a holster at her waist, practicing to make sure she could remove it and aim in an efficient, fluid gesture.

Opening the front door, she watched the dogs bound out ahead of her. The air was warm with just a slight breeze to cool it, and she could smell the smoke from a nearby fire. She scanned the tree line to make sure it wasn't a problem and saw it came from the direction of Amos's chimney.

Rachel walked the area where they had been that morning and the acreage beyond. A section she walked less frequently, it joined Hobart land, and she preferred to stay clear of him. The trees were gorgeous, especially at this time of year, but they also provided cover for any number of misdeeds. At least none grew close to the house. If someone came gunning for them, they would have some warning. *What a dismal thought*.

She tried to think of what she would make for supper. Many nights, it ended up being cereal or just raw vegetables, but she'd have to break the habit as she was losing weight and couldn't afford it. *Maybe soup.* It didn't take a lot of culinary talent to throw a few vegetables and some meat in a pot with water and spices.

The dogs had run ahead and she heard them suddenly bark, but it was the normal "I've found a squirrel" joyful bark, so she didn't run. As she cleared the trees, she saw them race forward to Seth's car, parked at the bottom of the steps. Glancing at her watch, she saw it was six p.m. already. Apparently, she had squandered two hours wandering in the trees.

Seth sat on the steps, a pizza carton balanced on his knees. He stood and lifted it away from the dogs' probing noses. "I brought a peace offering."

She stood there, trying to be mad, but the pizza smelled surprisingly good. “What kind?”

“Half triple cheese and tomato and half with pepperoni.”

“And which is my half?”

He looked relieved she hadn’t refused it out of hand. “Lady’s choice.”

“Triple cheese. I hate pepperoni.”

He stood back to let her walk in front of him. “Fair enough.” Taking a seat at the table, he watched as she dished out the dogs’ rations. “You walked earlier than usual today. Is everything okay?”

“Define okay.” She sighed. “Yes, it’s fine. The walls were just closing in.” The simple truth popped out before she had time to edit her words.

He nodded. “I get what you mean. It’s always been the most restful part of the day, and for now, that’s changed.”

“I hope it’s for now.”

Leaning down, he patted Jack who had settled at his feet. “We’re going to catch this bastard, Rachel. I promise.”

“Are you off duty?”

Looking confused, he nodded.

“I thought so.” Opening the refrigerator, Rachel reached in and handed him one of the cans of beer she’d bought at the grocery, taking one herself. “Pizza and beer on a Friday night is about as wild as I get.” She tried to smile, feeling awkward. Standing up, she opened one of the cupboards and withdrew two plates. Gesturing toward the box, she asked, “Two slices okay to start?”

“Sounds perfect.” He took a long swig. “Oh, that

tastes as good as it gets."

She slid his plate into the microwave, and when it was done, did the same things to hers. They ate in companionable silence. "So, where do you go from here as far as the investigation goes? Leaving the FBI out of it for now."

He finished his bite. "I still think our best bet is in the old file cases, but there's so much to go through. It takes a lot of time."

"Can't the others help you?"

"Not really," he answered. "The deputies are mostly handling everything else, and it's a lot of extra work for them. Wayne has done a lot of overtime, which has helped."

"How about me?"

He cocked his head. "I can't put you through something like that. There's some pretty graphic stuff in those files."

"Anything would be better than feeling so useless. I'm running around with a gun strapped to my hip, for God's sake, like some new-age gunslinger."

"Better to have it than wish you had." He scratched his chin. "I can't let those files out of my sight, and the people who gave them to me wouldn't approve of additional printouts. They already think I'm strange for preferring to work with hard copies of everything."

She glanced at her watch. It wasn't even seven o'clock. "Got a heavy date tonight, or do you want to find a killer?"

"No and yes, respectively."

"Well, we might have maybe four or five hours until fatigue sets in. Want to try?"

If Seth was shocked, he covered it well. "It's worth

a shot." He stood and made for the door. "I'll get the files and be back shortly."

"And I'll guard the pizza and chill a couple more cans of beer."

****

On the drive back to the station, Seth had a few minutes to ponder what the hell had just happened. He had gone to Rachel's expecting to get his ass kicked, and instead, she had offered to help him.

Women were confusing.

It made a strange kind of sense, though. She knew all the players except the copycat. She might even know him. Could she spot something he had missed? Or was she just hoping to avoid contact with the FBI?

The answer might be yes to both questions, but it didn't really matter. He had to try. The night dispatcher gave him a curious look as he waved and entered his office. It took just a minute to gather the files he'd printed out. He made it back out the door in four minutes flat.

Rachel opened the door as he climbed up the stairs and shut it behind him. "I'm surprised these weren't all e-files."

"They were." He set the heavy box on a spare chair. "I like hard copies. You go blind if you stare at a computer all of the time."

"True." She took the opposite seat. "What should I work through first?"

He had considered the options on the way back. "It might help if you examine all the victim profiles. The investigators never found anything they had in common except they were blondes and about the same age."

"Okay." She watched as he set a thick stack of

folders in front of her. "What are you going to look at?"

"Crime scene photos. I'm trying to anticipate his next move."

They settled in for a long evening.

****

Carson watched from the cover of the trees, cursing under his breath. What the hell was that Neanderthal sheriff doing at Rachel's place this late in the day? The bitch never has company, and she decides to break the rules tonight, of all nights, when he has precious cargo to deliver.

She ruined everything. Now slut number two would have to wait, wrapped up in the long toolbox of his truck, for another chance at the front page. That, or maybe he would wait a while. But staying in one place posed risks he couldn't take a chance on.

Tomorrow is another day.

****

Rachel stared across the room at Seth as he sprawled in the other recliner, sound asleep, a file propped on his chest. She couldn't decide whether she should wake him or not. The dogs lay between them instead of on their beds, as if they were confused about this unusual chain of events. *They aren't the only ones.* Sighing, she leaned to pull a throw over her legs. She could wake him at five a.m., which would leave him enough time to shower and change before work. Within minutes, she fell asleep.

She woke to find Seth staring at her, the dogs looking expectant. "What time is it?" she croaked.

"Five-fifteen in the morning." He leaned over, tightening the laces on his boots. "I need to go home and shower."

Her brain scrambled to catch up. "Were the victims natural blondes?"

"I don't know. Why?"

"Just trying to think out of the box." She shrugged. "That was one of the things that made my mother suspect my father, you know. All of a sudden, he wanted to dye my hair blonde."

He started to gather up the files. "I'll see if I can find out."

"Why don't you leave it with me?" She stood and stretched, feeling older than her age.

"I don't think it's such a good idea."

"Okay, how about this. Just leave the victim profiles with me. You have lots of other stuff to go through and your other sheriff duties to manage."

He paused, considering. "I'm covering tonight, but you can call me if you find anything that catches your eye."

She let him out into the early dawn. The dogs rushed after him, and she had to call them back. The three of them watched as his car headed down the long drive and through the trees. She waited while the dogs relieved themselves, then returned inside to dress up for their walk. The early air had a distinct chill.

Their walk happened without any problem, although the dogs seemed unusually tense, refusing to stray far from her side. She wondered if they knew something she didn't. Afterwards, she sat back down with the victim information. Poring over it just made her eyes fuzzy.

After a few hours, she received a text from Seth.

—All victims had dyed their hair. No natural blondes.—

It had to mean something, but what?
She sighed and sat back to give it more thought.

Chapter Eleven

After Seth sent the text to Rachel, he went home to grab some sleep before coming back to take the seven p.m.-to-seven-a.m. shift. One of his senior deputies had an out-of-town family funeral to attend, and since Seth wasn't getting much sleep with the murder hanging over his head, he figured he might as well cover the shift. Not much usually happened at night, mostly breaking up the occasional bar fight or the odd drunk driver.

He hoped it would be one of those nights.

Passing by Rachel's property about ten p.m., he watched as her lights switched off, all except her porch light. He didn't see anything out of the ordinary. By four thirty a.m., everyone in town looked to be at home except a few night workers whose vehicles he recognized. As he started back from the far side of town, his phone rang, and he picked up. "Sheriff Talbot."

"Seth."

Seth recognized Rachel immediately. "What's wrong?"

"I think I just saw movement down by the crime scene."

"Stay locked inside. I'm on my way. Five minutes." He shut off the phone, pulling a U-turn and scattering gravel in every direction. Speeding along the deserted road, his heart thumping with adrenaline, he ducked down the back road in the hopes of catching someone in the act. There were no parked vehicles. Before he left the car, he texted Rachel:

—I'm here. Trying to sneak in from the back road.—

He crept along the tree line, his nine-millimeter in his ready hand. A partial full moon gave him an additional glimmer of light. An owl hooted, and he almost swung the gun in that direction before his mind registered the origin of the sound. *Damn it*. The flashlight he held stayed pointed at the ground, so he wouldn't trip and give himself away.

Stopping, he listened for anything that didn't sound normal. All he could hear besides the owl was the soft breath of wind stirring the trees. He began to move again, working his way to the site.

Something soft and light fluttered from a tree branch. After peering at it, he thought he could make out a scarf, and he felt a heavy tug, deep in his gut. As he ventured closer, he smelled it; the deep, coppery scent of blood. Double-checking his surroundings, he knew he was too late and had missed his killer. Pointing his flashlight to give him added light, he called Rachel first. "I think he's gone, but I'm calling for more help. Stay inside."

Seth stood, casting his light into the depression, and right where the other victim had been was a new body. He couldn't see any details, other than the decisive shape and a note held down by a rock close to her head. Seth tried to push the crushing sense of failure away.

When he walked up the hill for better reception, he

heard the dogs set up a chorus of barks inside the house. Looking up, he could see Rachel standing by the window, her head in silhouette against the light, then she stepped away and the dogs quieted. First, he called Wayne, rousing him from sleep, telling him what equipment to bring. The younger man's excited voice meant he would arrive quickly.

A glance at his watch told him it was almost five a.m. The sun would be up in another hour, and that might help them a lot, but he wanted a closer look as soon as possible, which would only be possible with additional lights. He prayed for the slight chance of rain to stay away until they could investigate.

Seth saw Wayne's car approaching, and he waved a hand as he used the flashlight to illuminate his face. *That would be my luck to have my gung-ho deputy shoot me.* The squad car pulled beside him without incident. Wayne lowered the window. "Safe to park here?"

"Yes."

The other man put the car in park and stepped out. "How'd he get away so fast?"

"Damned if I know."

Wayne gestured toward the house. "Did she call it in or Amos?"

"She did." Seth pointed toward the trunk, which Wayne hustled to open. Inside were the floodlights he'd requested. "I'll wait until sunup for most of it, but these should let me get a quick look now." The two men dragged everything to a point twenty feet away from the body. "No closer. We can't take a chance on messing up any evidence."

Once it was set up, he put on gloves and ventured

closer, telling Wayne to stay back.

The young girl lay in the gully in what constituted a recurring nightmare for Seth. Same horrible gash as before, the blood dry. She was blonde, of course, but curvier and not as tall. He waved Wayne closer and showed him where to stand and take pictures, including one with the expected note in the same place as the first one. After the photos, Seth pried open the folded paper. The printing was oversize, almost exuberant in tone. It read, “She was fun, but there’s lots more where she came from.” Beneath those words, it said, “Say hi to Rachel for me.”

He cursed, trying to ignore the pounding headache which had started somewhere behind his eyes. Putting the note in a baggie, he handed it to Wayne and told him to turn off the lights and wait until dawn to continue. “I’ll call the coroner and tell him to come at first light.” Turning to leave, he added, “Stay by that tree and guard her remains. I’m going to talk to Rachel.”

She must have been watching, because as he approached the porch, the door opened. “Is it another body?”

He could see she already knew the answer by the bleak look on her face. “I’m afraid so.”

“Where’s the kid?”

“Wayne’s keeping watch. It’s almost light. We’ll continue our investigation then.” He rubbed a tired hand across his face. “What exactly did you see?”

“The dogs were just pacing around, growling, so I peeked out of the front window. All I could see was something hovering under the leaves.”

He nodded. “I think he left her there a while ago.

What you saw was a scarf he draped over a bough."

"Why didn't we hear him?"

"Maybe he came from a different direction. When did the dogs start fussing?"

She paused, looking thoughtful. "About ninety minutes ago, but they've been a little off all day."

"What do you mean, off?"

"On both of their walks, they wouldn't leave my side which is unusual. They didn't bark. They just seemed restless."

"Was Amos working close by?"

She shook her head. "He spent the morning fixing his tractor. His wife called earlier, just to check in."

He wondered for a moment if the dogs might have sensed someone watching. That made his stomach clench, but he didn't want to say anything to alarm her.

"Was there another note?"

"Yes."

"What did it say?"

He frowned. "He said it was fun." Now, he stared into her eyes. "And he said I should say hello to you."

She cursed, then shook her head as if to clear it. "How about I make a big pot of coffee?"

"We would appreciate that, Rachel." It would be better if she had something to keep herself occupied. He watched as she went inside.

Thirty minutes later, he had a mug of coffee and light had started to peek out around the edges. Dawn would arrive soon, so he called the coroner and wandered down to check on Wayne, armed with coffee for him, which he eagerly accepted.

"This is a learning opportunity for you, Wayne. I need you to watch how Doc works. He's very good at his job, and we need to help him in any way we can."

"Yes, boss."

Another thirty minutes later, the sun had begun to rise, and he spied the coroner's van entering the property. Two other vehicles followed and he frowned, recognizing a reporter from a nearby town in the first car. He strode up the hill, catching him as he exited. "No, sir. You can leave right now. This is private property."

"Sheriff, the people have a right to know." The reporter puffed out his chest, trying for an intimidating look. The people who had climbed out of the second car raised a camera and started snapping pictures.

Seth raised his voice and pointed down the hill. "None of you can come any closer than the outside of the gate. You have ten seconds to leave, or I'll charge you with trespassing."

Muttering, they climbed back into the cars and drove back down, leaving the vehicles partially blocking the gates. He didn't have time to fuss with them anymore. That would have to do.

The coroner parked where he had last time, and Seth followed him down the hill to the body.

He stood aside and let Doc do his job, content to see Wayne observing every step with interest. When the coroner was finished, his assistant prepared the body for transport to the morgue, and Doc came to stand beside him. "Poor thing. We don't see much of this kind of thing, do we, Seth? Thank God."

"Thought I left this carnage behind me when I escaped New York."

Doc shoved his hat back. "How is she doing?" he asked, gesturing toward Rachel's house.

"She's better than a lot of people would be under these circumstances."

Doc stepped a few extra steps away from Wayne and lowered his voice. "Do you think this has any connection to her father?"

The other man's comment left him speechless for a moment. "How do you know who her father is?"

"I've always known." He sighed. "It's a funny world. One of my best friends worked that case. I watched most of the trial play out, right there in the courtroom. Rachel, well, she always had a real way about her, even as a teenager."

"And you never told anyone."

He shook his head. "Just my wife. We figured the poor girl had experienced enough evil and deserved some peace."

"I appreciate that, Doc, and so would she."

"Thought I'd better mention it, but there won't be any holding back now. Everyone will find out. Even you can't protect her from this."

"I can try."

Doc leaned down and picked up his bag. He gestured down the driveway, toward the reporters' cars. "They'll figure it out by day's end. You'd better warn her." With that depressing statement, he headed for his van.

Seth and Wayne finished up, leaving the crime tape in place for the time being. He sent Wayne down to talk to the reporters. "Tell them nothing, except that I will give them an update on the situation at two o'clock at the station. Anyone entering any part of this property will be arrested for trespassing. After you talk to them, post yourself next to the crime scene until I say otherwise."

"Yes, boss." He strode down the hill.

Sick at heart, Seth headed for the house. As he approached, Rachel opened the door, looking pale. "Are those reporters?"

He nodded. "Let's go inside. They have long lenses on those cameras." Walking in, he greeted the dogs who gathered to mill at his feet. "Do they need to go out?"

Rachel shook her head. "I let them out back for a couple of minutes." She refilled the mug he'd returned and passed it back to him. "You need some sleep."

Shrugging, he replied, "What, dark circles and wrinkled clothes aren't my best look?" His feeble attempt at a joke prompted a distinct look of sympathy, which surprised him.

"What happens next?"

"We hope this autopsy gives us something more to work on."

"And if it doesn't?"

He took a deep breath and let it out, waiting for calm. It didn't come. "Doc thinks by nightfall, those assholes at the end of your drive are going to figure out who you are."

"You told the coroner?"

"Apparently, he already knew. A friend of his helped convict your father. He recognized you from the trial."

Now, she slumped into a chair. "You don't have any choice, do you? You're going to have to call the FBI for help."

"It's a question of manpower, Rachel. We're spread too thin as it is. There are other entities that could help, but because of the connection to your father, it should be the federal authorities." He leaned forward. "From now on, I need to be here every night if you'll let me."

"People will talk, you know."

"I don't give a damn about a bunch of busybodies with nothing better to do." Seth could tell he'd startled her by raising his voice, so he tempered the tone of it. "We need to catch him in the act. This jerk's getting more brazen by the second, and he'll make a mistake."

"He'll just see your car and stay away. You might have to consider that your overnight stay affected his timeline on this second murder."

Seth pondered for a moment. "That's a good point. I'll arrange for Wayne to drop me off at night and pick me up in the morning." He sighed. "In the meantime, I'm going to post Wayne here until suppertime. He can keep the news people at bay, and hopefully they'll get bored."

"I won't hold my breath."

He couldn't blame Rachel for her cynicism. "Did you need to go into town today for anything?"

She shook her head. "And I'll walk the dogs on the back acreage."

"That'll work." Seth picked up his mug. "Okay if I return this tonight? I need to get back to the office and make some calls."

Nodding, she stood and walked toward the door to open it for him. "Guess I'll see you tonight, Sheriff."

He noted the downgrade from his first name and wondered if she would ever forgive him for involving the FBI. "Okay, Rachel. See you then. Call me if you need anything." The door closed behind him. He noticed the cars hadn't left the end of the drive, although they were no longer blocking the exit. He met Wayne at the top of the hill. "I tried to get rid of them, Seth," Wayne said, frustrated. "They just said they'd wait and talk to you."

"Don't worry. I'll speak to them on my way out." He cursed under his breath at the intrusion. "Rachel will walk the dogs out back today, and otherwise she'll likely stay inside. Just make sure those idiots stay away from her and the crime scene."

The younger man nodded.

"I'll check in on you at noon. If I get too busy, I'll have Rosie run you up some lunch." He went to his car and drove down the hill. After a brief word with the press, repeating what Wayne had already said, he drove away, watching them cluster together in his rearview mirror. Hopefully, they would follow him back to town. When the news spread there had been a second murder, all hell would break loose.

Chapter Twelve

Seth made it as far as the property next door where he found Amos waiting on his tractor at the end of his driveway. Easing the car to a stop, he lowered the window. “What happened?” the farmer asked before Seth could say a word.

“Another girl. Same place as before.”

Amos’s expression spoke of sorrow. “But Rachel’s okay?”

“Yes. She saw something in the trees and called me, but we were too late to catch him.”

“She’s not safe there by herself. We tried to get her to come and stay with us.”

“I’ll tell you something, Amos. Just between you and me, okay?”

The other man nodded.

“Starting tonight, I’m going to stay in the house with her. I’ll have Wayne drop me off each night, so nobody can see my car.”

Amos looked shocked. “I’m surprised she gave her permission.”

“She wasn’t happy, but we have no choice. I’m worried she’s a target, and we don’t have enough staff to protect her.”

“You gonna call for some help?”

Seth sighed. “I have no choice, Amos. This is beyond what my department can handle.”

"Those feds will take right over. It's what they do."

Amos watched too much television, but Seth couldn't say that. "I have a friend who has worked with an agent who's better than most. We'll have to see if that person can come and help us out."

"Rachel won't want any part of their shenanigans."

Seth met the other man's gaze. "I'll do my best to take care of Rachel, but she's nobody's pushover."

"That's the truth of it," Amos said, restarting the tractor. "Still, I'll feel better, knowing you're holed up with her." With a wave, he turned and started down his driveway.

Seth continued to the office and shut off the ignition when he saw Rosie's worried face in the window. Premonition made his head ache. She met him at the door.

"What's wrong?" he asked. He should have asked what else is wrong, after the way the day had started.

"When I arrived this morning, some things were rearranged on my desk. I checked yours, and it looked different from the way you usually leave it." She grimaced. "The only person here, as far as I know, was Brady."

"What was he looking at?"

"Stuff about Rachel's background." She looked like she was about to cry. "I'm so sorry. Nobody's ever poked around my desk. I should have locked it all away."

Seth took a hold on his temper, with effort, wanting to throttle Brady. "Don't worry, Rosie. You shouldn't have to hide things from a co-worker. He's the one who's at fault." He took a calming breath. "Where is he?"

"He was supposed to check by the school this morning, but they said they haven't seen him."

"I'll take care of it." Seth jumped back into his car, driving past the school, where everything seemed to be normal at the start of the day. There was no sign of his problem deputy. He finally found the deputy's car parked in front of the Sammy's, the best breakfast joint in town. Seth stopped to check the glove box, and sure enough, there was Brady's duty gun, fully loaded. He took a second to remove the bullets, then stuck it in his car. On entering the restaurant, he caught sight of Brady, reared back in a chair, surrounded by locals. A member of his audience saw Seth first and called out, "Thought you'd be arresting that crazy bitch, Sheriff."

He came to a stop beside the table. Brady didn't even have the sense to stand up, instead letting all four chair legs hit the floor. "I'm not sure what crazy bitch you're referring to, Hooky."

"My crazy-ass neighbor with the killer daddy."

Seth stared at Brady, who smirked back at him. "You're fired."

The words brought him to his feet so fast his chair tumbled to the floor. "You can't fire me," he hollered, puffing out his chest like a bantam rooster.

"Just did." Seth turned and started for the door. When he reached for the handle, he turned. "Turn in your badge immediately. I already have your gun." As he went to his car, he thanked God the idiot had left the gun where he had. He knew Brady would follow him back to the office, which he did, actually roaring by him on the last turn, almost causing an accident. He leapt out of his car before Seth even shut off his engine, yelling, "You can't fire me just for stopping for breakfast."

They met, nose to nose, inside of the front door. "In my office," Seth said, through gritted teeth, as Rosie ducked into the copy room. "Now." He turned and led the way with Brady cursing a blue streak, storming after him.

"You can't—"

"Don't you tell me what I can and can't do. I'm in charge here, something you seem to forget."

"My uncle—"

"Aren't you getting a little old to have family members cleaning up after you, Brady?"

"You think you're such hot shit!"

Seth raised his eyebrows. "You're sitting on your ass when you should be working, leaking department matters to citizens, and sharing information you had no right to in the first place."

"The goddamn secretary has a right to it, and I don't?"

"That's right," Seth replied. "Your dubious work ethic kept you on the easiest assignments, and you still couldn't manage to do your job. And today, you left a loaded gun in an unlocked car where anybody could grab it. And, just to be clear, Rosie's a hell of a lot more than a secretary."

Brady offered a long string of profanity in answer.

"We're done here." Seth put a hand out and pointed to Brady's badge, which the other man threw on the desk in response. "Your check will be available in three days. You can pick it up then."

Brady slammed the door so hard when he left the glass rattled, letting a string of curses echo behind him.

A few minutes later, Rosie peeked around the

corner. “All clear on the battlefield?”

He nodded, waving her inside.

“Did he tell folks?”

“Yes, and he didn’t even have the sense to hide it.”

Her eyes opened wide. “What are you going to do?”

“With this second death, there won’t be any way to keep it under wraps. I’m going to call the FBI for help, and it’ll come out. I think they’ll be motivated because of the connection to their previous case.”

“Rachel won’t be happy.”

He grimaced. “She isn’t, but she knows I don’t have any choice. We just don’t have the manpower to take care of this.”

“Especially now.”

Seth nodded. “True enough, but Brady wasn’t doing much anyway, except causing trouble.”

“Well, the bad news is the mayor will probably call any minute now about Brady and the murder.” She smiled. “But the good news is Wayne’s cousin, Jeb, just completed cadet training. He got an offer from the city last week, but he hasn’t accepted it yet.”

Seth perked up. “Is he as smart as Wayne?”

She nodded. “Top of his class. Wayne was going to mention him to you, but he was worried it might be too pushy.”

“Do the two of them get along?”

“Like brothers.”

“Okay.” He thought for a minute. “Let me talk to Wayne about it. It might be an easy transition for us if it works out.”

After Rosie left, he reflected on the fact that she had offered the only bright spot in the day. Before lunch, the mayor called, steaming mad because Brady had told him he was fired for having breakfast on company time. When Seth informed him of the facts, including his casual mishandling of a loaded gun, he replied even he would be forced to give up on his sister's son.

So, at least that much was settled with less fuss than expected.

Doc had called to tell him the girl's corpse was two to three days old, just like the last one. Her basic description matched one of a local student who had gone missing a few days ago. They were just waiting for confirmation.

He looked at the mounting information, sighed, and picked up the phone. His friend gave him the agent's name in the Nashville branch of the FBI he found so helpful. Kind of sexist of him to be surprised it was a woman. Maybe it would help soothe Rachel's fears about the involvement of the feds.

And maybe not.

Agent Kendall James proved very efficient on the phone. She asked for copies of his files as soon as possible but noted that with the connection to Marcus Worth, she expected to get immediate approval for their assistance. He offered to clear out some space for them to work from this afternoon.

He assigned Rosie the task of tidying up and equipping their lunchroom which was the only space they had available. At least there were two large tables already there. They would bring laptops and cellphones with them, so other than electrical cords and a coffee machine, they should be all set.

Looking at his watch, he saw it read a few minutes

after one p.m. He hollered for Rosie, planning to send her out for lunch, but when she entered, she had a sandwich with two cookies in hand. She set them on his desk. “Don’t know what I’d do without you, Rosie.”

She smiled. “I figured you’d need some fortitude before you face the journalists.”

“That’s a nice term for a bunch of vultures.”

She cleared her throat. “Thought I’d better warn you there are at least two groups coming from the city and probably more on the way.”

He cursed. “Sorry, Rosie.”

“I was thinking the same thing, boss.”

“Can you take something to eat up to Wayne before they arrive?”

“I was going to, but he called, and apparently Rachel fixed him a sandwich and drink and brought it to him.” She raised her eyebrows. “Wayne said he hadn’t ever seen her close up, and he didn’t realize she was so pretty.”

Not pretty. Sexy. The thought flitted past, and Seth frowned. Like he didn’t have enough on his mind as it is. He told Rosie about his plans to spend the nights at Rachel’s house for the foreseeable future. She gave him a pointed look, which he ignored. “I’m only telling you and Wayne, so if something comes up, you’ll know where I am. Amos knows, too, just so he won’t worry.”

“I thought we had to consider Amos a suspect, just because of proximity and stuff.”

Seth smiled. “Amos might kill to protect his family, but I’d bet my life he’d never hurt a living thing otherwise.” He took a sip of his coffee. “I have pretty good radar about bad guys after New York.”

“What did the FBI have to say?”

"The agent said she'd look at the files, but she expected the go-ahead to come right away, because of the association with Dark Mark. I'd bet by tomorrow they'll be here." He tapped his fingers on the desk. "Can we have the room ready by quitting time?"

"Already done," she answered, heading for the door.

"You're the best."

"Yes, Sheriff," she answered, giving a mocking salute as she shut the door behind her.

Not an hour later, they were dealing with a ragtag bunch of strangers from the surrounding cities along with a few more local faces they recognized. They all shouted over top of each other, and he just stood quietly until they stopped, a tactic he'd learned in New York. "I have a short statement, and then I'll take questions as long as you don't yell so I can't hear you."

His statement covered the discovery of a second body, the name withheld, pending notification. He also mentioned the fact they were investigating the "potential" the two cases were connected.

"Is it true that one of your local residents, Rachel Mann, is the daughter of serial killer, 'Dark Mark' Worth?"

Seth had expected the question and knew it was supposed to catch him off guard. He swung to meet the gaze of the short, slender man with a ferret face. "I am here to protect the citizens of this county, Miss Mann included. Her family tree doesn't much interest me."

"Is Rachel Mann a suspect?"

This one came from a local woman who he recognized. "Now, Sarah Jean, you know everyone is a suspect until we have more information. Even you.

Miss Mann has been interviewed and has answered all of our questions in a helpful manner."

"Will the FBI be brought in?"

"The FBI is being consulted at this point."

One of the city reporters chimed in, waving her handkerchief for attention. I'd like to surrender myself, he thought, smothering an inappropriate grin. "Yes, ma'am."

"You said the two crimes shared similarities. Are they also similar to the Dark Mark crimes?"

Damn it. "At this point, we are just worried about our two crimes and protecting the citizens of this county. That's all for today, folks." He paused. "Actually, just one more thing. Anyone who ventures onto Miss Mann's property will be arrested for trespassing. No exceptions."

His comment elicited a babble of conversation and a few shouted complaints which he ignored, turning to re-enter the office building.

"That wasn't too bad," Rosie ventured, moving to peek through the blinds. "Most of them are headed out already."

"Tomorrow will be a lot worse, especially if the FBI shows up."

She shook her head. "It can't be helped."

"I might need some extra hours from you in the next few weeks."

"Extra work hours might frustrate the huge line of eligible men lined up at my door, but oh well." She chuckled. "No problem, Seth. Just tell me what you need and when."

"You're worth more than I can pay you, Rosie."

"True, but money's not everything." She went back

to her desk to answer the ringing phone. “May I ask who’s calling?” Her eyes widened, and looking at Seth, she mouthed the letters FBI.

He pointed toward his office, listening as she said, “One moment, I’ll connect you.”

Picking up the phone, Seth heard Kendall’s voice, confirming she and another agent would arrive mid-morning the next day. He outlined the arrangements they had made and the only addition they requested was a couple of extra desk lamps. He scribbled a note to remind himself and signed off.

Immediately after, Doc called and said the identity of their latest body had been confirmed and the parents would be notified within the hour. He sat and thought for a few minutes about how terrible it would be to lose a child in such a manner. Flipping open the victim’s file, he saw the missing person report. It had been made by her terrified parents after she failed to show up for a lunch date with her mother. The last place she’d been seen was a coffee shop where she stopped every morning. She never made it to her first class.

People, especially kids, never understood that being predictable could be dangerous. Easier to stalk you, easier to forecast a reliable timetable to use for planning. Killers liked habits. Women tended to get relaxed when they knew their surroundings. Too relaxed. Better to be a little paranoid, like him. Paranoia kept you safe.

Rachel had more than her share of paranoia and who could blame her. To be involved in murder not once, but twice, stretched anyone’s sense of credibility. He thought about that one reporter’s question, “Is Rachel Mann a suspect?” Technically, she was, to be sure, but the inherent sadness in her eyes convinced him she wasn't involved. The idea of tainted blood was overblown. In his experience, plenty of monsters had perfectly normal family members.

Chapter Thirteen

Seth glanced at his watch, startled to see it was already after four p.m. "Rosie," he called. After a minute, she poked her head in. "Head home early tonight. Tomorrow's going to be a much longer day, and we all need sleep."

She nodded. "Okay, but how about you?"

"I'll catch some sleep tonight."

"What, propped in a chair, with only a loaded gun for company?"

He grinned. "She's got a couple of dogs to warm my feet, anyway."

"You need me in early tomorrow?"

He shook his head. "Be prepared to stay late, though. I'm pretty sure it's going to blow up tomorrow."

"Will do."

After she left, Seth checked in with his other deputies and headed out to Rachel's. He was happy to see the news people had cleared off. Wayne walked along the crest of the hill, looking down on the crime scene.

He pulled over next to him, lowering the window. "Any problems?"

Wayne shook his head. "No. Only one of the news guys came back after you spoke to them, and when he saw me still here, he left."

"The short, slender one with the rodent face?"

"How'd you know?"

Seth sighed. "He's going to be a problem. I can always smell them a mile away." He shrugged. "Rosie said Rachel brought you some lunch."

The younger man smiled. "She was right nice about it, too. The dogs growled at me at first, but then they calmed down. I didn't think she was unfriendly at all, just quiet."

"Rosie told me about your cousin, Jeb."

Wayne flushed, the color reaching his ears. "I was going to mention him, but I didn't want to be pushy."

"Did you hear I fired Brady?"

"Yes, Sheriff." Seth noted he looked pleased. "I know it leaves you short-handed, but I'll work all the overtime you need."

"Appreciate it, Wayne. If I find your cousin acceptable, do you think you would work well with him?"

The man's grin lit up. "Yes, sir. We work great together."

"You think he can come in and see me sometime tomorrow? If his marks are as good as Rosie says and his instructor's opinion is solid, he might fit in well here. But you just tell him to come see me tomorrow if he can." Seth tried, and failed, to visualize his schedule. "Let Rosie know when he's available. He might have to wait a while, because it's going to be crazy busy, but we need more bodies on the job. Might be baptism by fire as they say, but he'll learn quick."

Wayne said he would, and Seth asked him to go to his house with him and wait while he threw together some fresh clothes to take to Rachel's. His deputy peppered him with questions about the case, offering a few insights even more seasoned officers might have missed. If Jeb was half as good as Wayne proved to be, Seth would be pleased.

When they returned to Rachel's, he had Wayne drop him at the back of the house in case anyone was watching. Warned by his text, Rachel let him in, giving a half-hearted response to Wayne's wave.

"You made friends with my deputy."

"The kid had to eat something."

He watched as she walked across the room to switch off her computer. "Did I interrupt you?" She seemed a little cranky, and he watched as she paced to the window. "The vultures are gone for now."

Turning, she tried to smile. "So, I'm not the only one who thinks of them that way."

"Hell, no." He set his bag down, watching as the dogs sniffed it with enthusiasm, tails wagging. "Journalists are the bane of law enforcement. They have screwed up more cases than anyone alive."

"Did my father's name come up when you spoke to them?"

No way to avoid this one. "Yes," he answered, trying for nonchalance. "I told them you are a citizen of this county, and I don't care about your family tree."

"They won't let it go."

"I know." Walking forward, he touched her arm, as a test. She didn't jerk away, but he felt her tense. "We'll handle each day as it comes. You have more friends here than you know."

"You and Wayne?" She rubbed her face and he noticed the circles around her eyes.

"Amos and Edith." He cleared his throat. "And you

can add Doc and Rosie to the mix. They're both good people you can rely on."

"They always say hello at the grocery store, at least. More than can be said for a lot of folks."

He swore. "I meant to stop and pick up some groceries."

She gestured toward the refrigerator, and he opened it. The shelves were mostly full and not just with vegetables. Seth could see more beer and the makings for tacos in front. He raised his eyebrows.

"I figured this was where we might be headed with this mess, so I asked Edith to pick up a few things for us and have Amos drop them off. We can have stew tonight, tacos tomorrow, if that works."

He shrugged out of his jacket. "My stomach thanks you. I'll pay you back."

"I'm not worried. If you catch this asshole, I'll buy you groceries for life."

"Watch what you promise. I eat a lot."

"You work long hours, so you need fuel." She looked at her watch. "Dinner's in the crock pot. It'll be ready in about an hour. I need to take the dogs out."

"I'll come with you."

"What if someone sees you?"

"We can stay out back, and it's not dark yet. Amos is the only one who would see us this early, and he knows I'm staying here."

"He does?"

Seth nodded. "He and Edith are really worried about you, and he already has enough concerns, watching out for his children."

"That's true."

"Don't worry. He won't tell anyone."

She chuckled with a semblance of real humor. “Not like I have a pristine reputation to live up to.”

“Me, either.”

They watched in silence as the dogs gamboled in front of them, racing after a rabbit until Rachel called them off. After thirty minutes, they returned to the house. As they opened the door, a rich, meaty smell replaced the cooler air, and he realized how hungry he felt. She fed the dogs and he dished up the stew, grabbing the loaf of French bread and a butter dish from the counter. A can of beer showed up by his plate when he stood up to fetch the paper towels. “Thanks,” he said, popping it open. “Just one tonight, so I don’t drift off.”

“Have to sleep sometime. We can take shifts.”

“Call me old-fashioned if you want, but I’m the one standing guard.”

She shrugged. “Okay. My gun is on the top shelf of the closet. After what happened the other night, I’m keeping it loaded and ready if you ever need it.”

“Mine are right here”—he pointed to the holster on his hip—“and here.” He lifted his pants leg to show a smaller gun at his ankle.

“Hmmm. I always thought ankle holsters were just for cops on television.”

He shook his head. “That little sucker has saved my bacon, more than once.”

They dished up the food and sat, sharing a surprisingly comfortable silence while they ate. He swallowed his bite. “This is really good.”

“Don’t sound so surprised,” she replied.

“Do you cook a lot?”

“Mostly, I’ll prepare a dish and just eat the same

thing for three or four days. How about you?"

Seth laughed. "I pretty much think I'm a chef if I can grill a couple of steaks without burning them." He watched the dogs milling around, looking hopeful.

"Nope," Rachel said, and sighing, they went and lay down.

It made him chuckle. "Do you ever feed them from the table?"

"No. They get too moochy if you do. And people food is too rich for them, anyway." Standing, she reached for his plate. "Want some more?"

"Absolutely." Rachel handed him another serving, but he noticed she put her dish in the sink. "You're not having more?"

"If I ate like you, I'd be as big as a house." She blushed at the sound of her words. "No offense. I just meant women don't seem to be able to eat the way men can without gaining too much weight."

"Glad I'm a man, then. I'm pretty much always hungry." He gestured toward the dogs. "Where did you get these two?"

She frowned. "Some idiot dumped them in the ditch by the front gate. They were only five weeks old, according to the vet."

"That's too young to be away from their mama."

"I don't think whoever left them gave a damn."

You did, though. You didn't give them away or take them to the humane society. Aloud, he said, "They seem pretty happy here."

She patted Zack's head when he came to lay it on her knee. "They're excellent company. And they make a good alarm system, although I'm not sure they would tear a bad guy to pieces."

"Give you enough time to grab your gun, though."

"Exactly." She stood and tidied the dinner dishes while he finished his second serving. He carried his plate and silverware to the sink, rinsed them, and put them in the dishwasher.

"Guess your mother raised you right," she commented.

He smiled. "My mother would have tanned my hide if I didn't do my share."

"Were you close to your folks?"

The memories raised by her question brought happiness, not pain. "Yup. I was about as lucky as you can get when it comes to parents." He remembered her situation had been so different and winced. "Sorry."

"Don't be." She met his gaze. "I had a great mom. She did her best until she just couldn't anymore."

Now, Seth felt awkward. "You just go about your evening ritual. I don't want to interfere."

Rachel laughed, which made the dogs wag their tails. "Our ritual is to watch television until we start to drift off."

"Sounds good to me."

They moved into the den area where she chose one of the chairs, leaving the couch to him. The confused dogs chose a spot between them to hunker down. She tossed him the remote, and he picked a comedy, figuring they could all use a little laughter. Two hours later, she headed back into the kitchen, and, as if reading his mind, poured a glass of soda and shook some chips into a bowl, dropping it off beside him.

Where has the prickly recluse gone, he thought, surprised. Right at this moment, it seemed like any easy evening between friends. She let the dogs out at ten for a few minutes, then brought out some bedding and wished him goodnight.

He sat there a few minutes, pondering the change in their circumstances, then pulled out the folders of information to look through. About three thirty, he gave in to fatigue and took a nap.

Chapter Fourteen

Rachel woke at five thirty a.m. and went to wake Seth, finding him slumped amid the spread of papers. A few minutes later, Wayne picked him up at the back door, and they both waved goodbyes.

Well, that was weird.

It hadn't been as uncomfortable as she expected, which was strange. She figured any other woman he spent the night with probably had an entirely different reaction. In her limited experience, men like him were the very reason the term "getting lucky" had come into existence.

But that was beside the point.

Bundled in a raincoat against the faint spray of raindrops they had been warned were coming, she took the dogs out at six a.m. Glad she had done her errands earlier in the week, she planned a quiet day inside. As they mounted the steps, she heard a rumble of thunder. A half an hour later, the skies opened. The pummeling on the metal roof gave her an odd sense of comfort. Heavy rains would likely keep news people and bad guys away.

Late morning, she received a text from Seth. It read "Everything quiet?"

"Fine," she answered, not knowing what else to say.

In the afternoon, the rains let up, and Rachel

prepared the tacos ahead of time and, covering them in plastic, put them back in the fridge. She thought she might take the dogs out until she glanced out and saw a car parked at the end of her drive. A man stood beside it, a pair of binoculars in his hand.

Come on in—I dare you. I have a couple of four-legged friends who will tear the ass out of those suit pants in a heartbeat.

Much to her relief, he left after about an hour. Right away, her cellphone began to ring, about every ten minutes. She didn't recognize the number. This was how it started, she remembered, the endless haranguing from journalists, who were sure they had a right to know.

What about my rights?

Rachel turned the volume down and called the dogs to follow her. Staying close to the house for a change of pace, she threw a ball for them for what seemed like hours, judging by the fatigue in her arm. They loved the fuzzy, yellow tennis balls, but she went through a bucket every month, because they liked to chew them, too. As long as they didn't eat them, she figured their pleasure was worth the expense.

Rachel glanced at the clock and saw it read a few minutes after six. Surprised Seth hadn't shown up yet, she wondered when to warm up the tacos. Groaning at how domestic it all seemed, Rachel checked her phone and found a text from Seth.

—I'll be a little late; closer to seven.—

She texted back—*Okay*—and wondered what kept him.

When she heard arrival sounds, a different engine from Wayne's patrol car disturbed the quiet. Glancing out the front, she saw a big black SUV prowling up the drive. Past them, she saw the newsman's car from the morning parked down by the gate. *Terrific.* If she was right, that SUV held an FBI agent or two, and some journalist waited there to keep track of their visit.

Gone were her dreams for another uncomplicated night. The dogs set up a warning chorus of howls, and just for spite, she let them out to greet the car. They milled around it, growling, until Seth climbed out. Their wagging tails spoiled her fun, and she watched as a woman stepped down from the driver's seat and stopped to pat Jack.

Traitor, she thought as the dog rubbed his head against the other woman's hand.

Her visitors headed up the stairs, giving her just enough time to register the petite blonde stature of the agent. Not exactly what she had been expecting.

Seth knocked, and Rachel opened the door to let them in, calling the dogs.

"Sorry, we're late."

"You hardly have to punch a time clock, Sheriff." Rachel knew she was being bitchy. She just didn't care.

"Rachel, this is Special Agent Kendall James."

She leaned forward and shook the agent's hand, finding it firm and efficient. The other woman's eyes seemed to measure her every move, but then she smiled. "I'm sorry for the intrusion, Miss Worth."

Rachel stiffened. "It's Mann, Agent James. My last name is Mann."

"Of course. My apologies." The look in her eyes said she was anything but sorry. Rachel knew they did these things as of a personal test of whoever they were interviewing, but that didn't make it less offensive. She turned, and going to the refrigerator, poured herself a glass of water to give herself time to cool off. She didn't offer her visitors anything.

"I thought I would drop the sheriff off tonight, so we could meet."

"Oh?" Rachel took a drink. "And exactly why is that important?"

The other woman smiled, teeth gleaming. "We're all working together to figure out what's going on." She patted Seth's arm. "I told Seth he doesn't need to spend his nights here. If the situation merits, I can stay."

"No."

"I beg your pardon?"

Rachel sucked in a breath. "This is still my house. I made room for Seth, but the invitation doesn't extend to you or anyone else. Period."

"There's no need to make this unnecessarily awkward." The agent tapped her fingers on the table as if to make a point.

Rachel snorted. "It's already awkward. My house. My rules."

"No problem, Rachel," Seth interrupted, clearly gauging her temper. "Agent James wanted to meet you and assure you they will be as unobtrusive as possible." He glanced toward the front window. "How long has the journalist been here?"

"He was here for about an hour earlier. He's been there tonight for almost an hour. I know because he wasn't there when I took the dogs out."

"He might back off if you give him a brief statement," Kendall suggested.

"That will never happen." Rachel had no intention of giving them any more fodder for the mill, and she didn't care who thought it was a great idea.

"I knew your father," Kendall offered, clearly trying to throw her off guard.

Rachel peered to look down on the agent. "Good for you." She took another drink of the water she still held. "How old were you at the time—ten?"

The other woman laughed. "I was a brand-new agent, all of twenty-four, but thanks for the compliment."

Rachel felt a grudging admiration the agent didn't seem angry or put off by her attitude. "So, you were just invited as a go-along to watch the big boys work?"

"More or less."

"And what was your take on the esteemed Professor Worth?"

"That he was the worst of the worst. Someone with absolutely no conscience who had the looks and the brains to fool almost anyone." She smiled. "He solidified my commitment to my job. After the investigation, I felt the focus of my career should be to stop men like him."

Rachel was silent for a moment, reassessing.

"I'm not the enemy, Rachel."

She took note of the softening of Kendall's voice.

"My partner and I are here to assist Seth. We will work together to get this bastard thrown in jail where he belongs."

"How?"

Kendall sighed. "We're working it out. Tonight, Bill, my partner, and I will go over all the files and work out the best way to proceed. We will be sure to warn you ahead of time about anything that affects you. Okay?"

Rachel nodded.

"I do have one request."

"What?"

"I'd like you to wear a protective vest when you go outside."

Rachel opened her mouth to voice a protest and then shut it again to reconsider. *How stupid would she look if the bastard shot her and it could have been prevented?* "It won't protect my head."

"I know, but most gunmen shoot for the torso as I'm sure you're aware. I can hardly ask you to stay inside for the foreseeable future. You'd go stark raving mad. So would I." The agent stood.

"I guess that's a reasonable request."

"Good. The vest is in the car. I'll give it to Seth when he walks me out." She rubbed her hands together. "Well, back to work for me. One of you call if anything pops up." She opened the door, and Seth trailed after her.

Rachel watched through the window as Kendall reached into the back of the SUV and pulled out a vest, handing it to Seth. It occurred to her as she watched them that they looked like the perfect couple, his brawn to her petite femininity. She snapped the drapes shut and went to sit down, pretending she hadn't spied on them. After a few minutes, he re-entered the house, draping the vest on the back of the chair.

"Is the newsman still there?"

Seth shook his head. "Sun's setting, so he's probably headed back to whatever hole he crawled out from." He sniffed the air. "We're still on for tacos?"

Nodding, she stood and fetched him a beer, in what suddenly seemed like a very familiar move. Waving him to a chair, she slapped it down with a little too much force.

"What did you think of Agent James?"

She knew better than to trust the casual tone of the question. "She's no worse than any of the others."

"Her record is impeccable."

"Bully for her." She heard the bitchy tone, and this time, regretted it. "Look, I'm sure she'll do the best she can. And I know you need the help." Watching as he flipped open the can of beer, she reached up to lift their plates out of the cupboard. "I don't have to like it, though. I know most people think my life is boring as hell, but I like it just fine. I don't care for a crowd of folks underfoot."

"Me, either."

Surprised, she sat down across from him, setting the plates on the table. "You're kidding, right? Mr. Popular, former football star from high school and every girl's dream. You attract a crowd everywhere you go."

He shrugged. "I like people just fine, but at the end of the day, I want quiet. Most of the people I've dated don't appreciate a good home-grilled steak and a movie like I do."

"That surprises me. Not about other people, but about what you prefer."

A chuckle followed his gulp of beer. "And how do you know I played football?"

"The little girl at the grocery store has a king-size crush. She babbles on about you all the time."

He looked horrified. "Patti Sue? She's half my age. I went to school with her aunt, for heaven's sake."

His reaction made her laugh. "I guess you're close

enough in age as far as she's concerned. Wouldn't matter to a lot of men."

"It matters to me," he replied. "It's hard enough to find someone your own age you have things in common with."

Suddenly uncomfortable, she stood and grabbed the oven mitts, sliding the tray of tacos out of the oven. The dogs stood up and wandered over, sniffing. Her reprimand sent them back, grumbling, to their beds.

Rachel dished a couple of tacos onto each plate and slid one in front of him. "Lots more where they came from," she said and took a testing bite. The cheese and tomato combination was her favorite part, but the rest didn't taste bad, either. She ate two to Seth's six, understanding the hum he made as he ate likely constituted approval.

Sitting back with a sigh, he wiped his mouth with the napkin. "That was heaven."

"Pie for dessert."

He raised an eyebrow. "What kind?"

"Peach and I bought vanilla ice cream to go with it if you want."

Seth paused, considering the options. "Let's wait an hour and then we can have both."

She smiled. "The dessert's for you. I don't like either one."

Disbelief lit his eyes. "Who doesn't like ice cream and pie?"

Rachel moved into the den and sat in her chair. "I usually only eat chocolate ice cream and a good cookie, preferably with chocolate chips in them. Do you sense a theme here?"

Following her, he plopped with a sigh onto the

couch. "What is it with women and chocolate? Lots of great desserts aren't chocolate."

"Believe it or not, there are already too many great choices with chocolate. Adding too much of anything else would likely make my heart explode and then, boom, game over."

He leaned down to pat Zack's head, giving it a rub. "So, you have a monster bag of cookies hidden away and your freezer's full of ice cream."

She shook her head. "I don't usually keep sweets in the house. Too tempting. On the weekend, I wander down to that ice cream place on Main street and have a sundae or a milkshake and take one of their big cookies home with me."

"That's it?"

His disbelief made her smile. "That's why I walk twice a day. So I can afford those weekend calories."

Seth chuckled. "I'd die of starvation on those rations." Picking up the television control, he switched it on. "What do you feel like watching tonight?"

She realized, at least for a while, she'd forgotten all about the FBI. The inclination to thank him for the respite passed, because she didn't want the mood to shift. "Let's find something funny." They switched back and forth between programs until ten, when she stood up to let the dogs out.

The night passed much the same as before, other than the fact she spent an inordinate amount of time thinking about him lying on the couch. He wasn't just another pretty face, she realized. It might have been better for her if he fit into some preconceived box. The unsettling thought had her tossing and turning all night.

But after Wayne picked him up in the morning, she

missed him. *What the hell is that all about?* She never missed anybody, except the dogs. This was the problem with people, she thought, shoving the chair out of her way as she headed for the front door. *People complicate everything.*

Rachel paused to add the vest and her holstered gun, feeling rather over-dressed. Whistling for the dogs, she stood aside as they raced out the door, and she slammed it behind them. Maybe a walk would clear this bullshit out of her head.

****

Carson watched through the binoculars. Rachel headed out to the back field, as she had for the last several days. Did she think a simple change of direction would keep her safe? The idea made him chuckle. How could this country bumpkin have sprung from the loins of a genius like Marcus Worth?

He should have been the heir apparent, a murderer by the virtue of having inherited the same drives. He and Marcus had been brought together by destiny. What a shame some thug had shortened his mentor's lifespan, before he had the chance to witness their remarkable plan come to fruition.

Rachel had always been the ultimate target, the other foolish bitches just a warmup for the main event. It seemed only fitting Carson would now carry out the final wish of Marcus Worth…

To kill his arrogant bitch of a daughter.

He pulled back under the cover of the trees. With profound sadness, he realized it was time to leave. The sun edged over the hills and his observation would be further compromised by the jaded journalists, determined to find a story.

Oh, he'd give them a story about Rachel, although perhaps not the one they expected. He cut through the trees and, climbing the fence, found his way back to the truck, parked on Hobart land. Although the farmer on the far side of Rachel's patrolled his land like a sentry, her other neighbor spent most of his time belching in front of the television, wrapped around a can of beer, making access to his acreage remarkably easy. Whistling, Carson opened the door and, climbing in, started the engine and began to make plans.

Chapter Fifteen

Kendall looked up as Seth entered the police station. “When do you plan to sleep, Sheriff?”

Seth frowned. “At the moment, I catch a few hours here and there.”

“You need your sleep.”

“What I need is to protect the folks that count on me.”

“Like Rachel?”

He took note of the measuring attitude in her gaze. “Rachel is one of many citizens who count on us to protect them. They aren’t used to psychos like this.” He realized the irony of his words and clarified. “For her, one psycho per lifetime is more than her share.”

“Well, Bill and I are used to psychos. And I know in your former work in New York, you’ve seen a lot more than you do here.”

“That’s true.” He smiled and pulled out a chair to sit in, reaching out a hand as Rosie approached, out of habit. Rosie passed him his messages and kept walking, murmuring, “Morning, boss,” under her breath.

“Do you ever miss it?”

He raised an eyebrow. “Why the fifth degree?”

“You were a very successful officer, advancing far more quickly than average. It just seems like…”

“A waste?”

She nodded. “No offense intended.”

"None taken." He poured himself some coffee and topped hers off. "This is where I grew up. It's where I always intended to return. Kind of hard to explain to a city girl."

"Guilty as charged." She took a sip. "Well, you could always find a job with the bureau if you were so inclined. Your experience would be invaluable."

"Good to know." He never would, and he figured she knew it, but it was a nice invitation, regardless. "Did you and Bill see anything in the files we need to discuss?"

She shook her head. "It's just like you said. There isn't much to work with. We would like to have a look around Rachel's place if possible. Why don't we do it later on in the day, and then we'll just leave you there when we head back to the hotel."

"That'll work."

She tapped her index finger on the file folder. "We wanted to ask Rachel a few questions about her father to get a better feel. Do you think she'll co-operate?"

"Just be tactful. She's really bright, but she doesn't like games." He narrowed his gaze to make a point.

"I know. Yesterday, I wanted to see how quick she is to anger." She shrugged. "I actually liked her. She's a little hostile, but who wouldn't be under these circumstances."

"Bill doesn't seem too pushy."

She shook her head. "Nah, he's the good cop in our team. But he's really quick to read people and has lightning reflexes. Those skills count for a lot in this business." They made plans to meet back at the station at four o'clock and then went in their separate directions. Seth talked to Wayne about some issues they were having with a group of teenagers hassling younger kids. Afterwards, he looked at the stack of messages from journalists. How many times could someone say, "We're working on it?" He compromised by telling them to show up for a briefing tomorrow afternoon. Hopefully, it would stave them off for now.

After lunch, he found a tall, stocky, young man waiting in the front seating area, running a restless hand through dark hair. Waving Rosie inside his office, he asked if their visitor was Wayne's cousin, Jeb. "Yes," she whispered. "Do you want me to see if you can get his instructor on the phone? I know you haven't had time to call him yet."

He sighed. "Can you just get me the number, and tell Jeb it's going to be a few minutes."

"Sure. I already looked it up." She returned with it in a flash and shut the door as she exited.

Seth had a turn of luck for a change and found the training officer eating a sandwich at his desk, happy to talk to a fellow policeman. He confirmed Wayne's cousin had indeed placed first in his class and gave him an enthusiastic referral. Seth thanked him and ended the call. After a moment, he asked Rosie to send the young man in.

Jeb entered, baseball cap in hand, taking the opposite seat when Seth waved him to it. There wasn't much resemblance between him and Wayne other than height, but Jeb looked him straight in the eye and waited for him to speak.

"Thank you for coming so quickly."

He flushed. "It's a pleasure to be asked, sir."

"We're down a man, and I'm sure you're aware we have a big problem right now."

"Yes, sir. Wayne filled me in, and, well, everyone's talking about it."

Seth nodded. "Your instructor spoke highly of you and that means a lot, but it's really important to me you're a team player. We're a small department, so getting along with people is more essential here than it might be in a larger city."

"Yes, sir. I like helping people. That's one of the reasons I decided on law enforcement for a career."

"And you want to remain in this area? I know you've already had an offer from Nashville."

The younger man nodded. "That's why I was happy when Wayne mentioned this possibility, sir. I have to make a decision soon, but I love this county and I know it inside out, like you do. Staying here would be my first choice."

"With what we have going on here, it's going to be baptism by fire." He trusted his gut on this. "You'd have to start right off the bat, working a lot of overtime. It's what we're all doing right now."

"No problem, sir."

Seth liked the shine of enthusiasm in Jeb's face and hoped it wouldn't wear off too soon. "Did Wayne give you an idea about compensation and benefits?"

"Yes, sir."

Seth nodded. "Okay, Rosie's going to give you a package that spells all of the information out for you. Read it carefully, and ask her any questions you like. If you're content with it all, sign the papers, and you have yourself a job."

"Gosh, sir. That's great." He reached out and shook Seth's hand, pumping it like a piston.

"How soon can you start?"

"I'm ready now if you need me, sir."

Seth smiled. "If you can stay and fill out all your paperwork and get your identification rolling, we should be all set to start tomorrow morning. Eight thirty sharp, young man."

"Yes, sir." Seth waved Jeb out and handed him off to Rosie. She gave a big thumbs-up as he closed the office door. Maybe, just maybe, this bit of good luck would turn the tide. Finding someone to hire sometimes took months, so he felt grateful Jeb seemed like a good fit.

The rest of the day passed by in a flash. Seth realized if he kept gulping coffee at this rate, he'd have a state-sized hole in his stomach from all the acid. Lunch was a sandwich at his desk. After he finished, he warned Rosie about his plan to take a power nap for thirty minutes and laid his head back, closing his eyes. An old habit from precinct days, it filled the void when homicide cops might work for three days straight with little rest.

Before Seth could blink, it was four p.m. He and the agents headed up to Rachel's with Bill at the wheel. The slender, black-haired man didn't say much, but his gaze seemed to absorb everything around him. Kendall had referred to him as a human computer, which made Seth wonder if he would notice something Seth hadn't. When they turned in the drive, Kendall said, "Should we warn Rachel we're here?"

"I already did," Seth answered. "I texted her this afternoon." He didn't miss the glance passing between the two agents. "She's more relaxed with a little warning."

Bill nodded, and they exited the vehicle. First, Seth

showed them the valley where the bodies and first notes had been found, then they walked to the upper side where the sniper's nest waited and the other note had been located.

"Tell us a little more about the neighbors, please." It was the first words Bill had spoken all day.

Seth paused and turned to gaze downhill. "Well, on the lower side is Amos and his family. Long-time farmers, good people, three young kids."

"How young?"

"Too young to be involved in this. Oldest is fourteen, I think, the youngest about four."

The other man nodded. "How about the folks on this side?"

"Hooky Hobart, early forties, unmarried. Terminal lazy ass, inherited the farm, which he's letting fall apart. Spends most of his days drinking and whining."

"Do he and Miss Mann get along?"

Seth failed to stifle his laugh. "No, sorry. Hooky thinks Rachel is a freak and loves to speculate about what a woman does here alone. I think he might have made a pass at her and didn't like her response."

The other man narrowed his gaze. "What was her response, do you know?"

"My assistant said she told him to lace his shorts a little tighter and keep walking, or words to that effect." Seth put a hand out toward the other man. "You'll have to trust me on this one. Hooky doesn't have the brains or the energy to pull all this together."

"Do you mind if we talk to him?"

He smiled. "I'd be thrilled, actually. He's a pain in the ass."

"It might be better for everyone concerned if Miss

Mann stayed inside for the time-being."

Seth sighed. *No way she will.* "She stays pretty much put most of the time, but I think she gets a little stir-crazy."

"It's the only way to keep her safe." Intensity lit Bill's face.

Seth nodded. "And she knows that. But she's been through this before and wants to feel like she can protect herself."

"What kind of plan does she have in place?"

"She has two dogs who are a good warning system and a licensed gun she knows how to handle."

The agent looked skeptical. "Are you trusting her word or have you seen her shoot?"

He shook his head. "Amos vouched for her. Apparently, they have practiced together at the back of his place, and she's an excellent shot, even better than him. His word is good enough for me."

"Okay." Bill scrawled a note in his pad. "We'll talk to both of them tomorrow." He took a final glance around. "Shall we head up to the house?"

Bill moved the SUV to the front steps, and as he did, the dogs swarmed from the rear of the house, barking, staying level with the vehicle until it came to a stop. Jack made a beeline when he saw Seth closing in, but Zack stayed at the driver's door, growling. Bill stayed closed inside.

"Once they get a smell of him, they should be okay," Seth offered, as Rachel joined them.

Kendall chuckled. "Yeah, well, Bill's not too fond of dogs. Do you think they could stay outside until we're done?"

Rolling her eyes, Rachel called them off and made

them lie down. Bill exited the car, his reluctance evident in every tentative step. He edged past the dogs and hustled up the stairs, leaving the others to follow as they smothered grins.

Inside, he glanced around as if searching for intruders.

"Sit," Rachel said, in the tone she normally used on her dogs. She waved a hand at the chairs. The agents followed her suggestion, introducing Bill as they sat down.

Seth gestured toward the refrigerator. "Rachel, do you mind if we have a cold beer?"

"Help yourself," she replied.

Bill smiled for the first time all afternoon. "It's end of day. I think I'd go for one."

"Kendall?"

"A glass of ice water would work for me. Thanks."

Rachel moved to reach for two glasses, filled them with ice and tap water, and handed one to Kendall. Seth figured it was the only peace offering Kendall was likely to see today. He grabbed a beer for him and Bill, passing it across the table.

Rachel didn't let time pass. "What is it you want to know? I would have thought all of the endless stack of files would have given you the goods on my father."

Bill leaned forward, his intense gaze a little intimidating. "We have a lot more on his victims than we actually do on your father. To be honest with you, we would likely have never caught him if it weren't for your mother's bravery."

Oh, he was smart, Seth thought, this unassuming agent with the searching eyes. It would be stupid to underestimate him. Appealing to Rachel's love for her mother might help ease this situation.

Rachel nodded. “I wish she could have seen herself as the hero. I think she thought she was stupid for not figuring it out sooner.”

“Anyone in this situation would feel the same way. They believe thinking someone they love is evil makes them disloyal, but instinct is a powerful thing.” He leaned forward, meeting Rachel’s gaze. “How would you describe your father?”

Seth could see the question surprised her. She took a moment to consider. “Handsome, arrogant, charismatic, selfish…empty.”

Kendall spoke up, voicing the question everyone was thinking. “Empty in what way?”

Rachel rubbed her face; a move Seth knew signaled frustration. “I don’t know. Maybe that’s the wrong word. I just mean nothing ever touched him. He never seemed happy or sad or anything, really, except smug.”

“A true sociopath,” Kendall interjected. “He knew what he did was wrong. He just didn’t care.”

Bill tapped his fingers on the table. “What kind of a relationship did the two of you have?”

“We didn’t.” Rachel took a sip of water. “He was the handsome man who sometimes ate dinner with us. My mother did everything for me. In the beginning, she made excuses for him, then afterwards, she just gave up.”

“Did he ever bring anyone home with him, like a guest or a friend?” Bill scrawled a note and looked up.

Rachel shook her head. “He used to say nobody could entertain him better than he could entertain himself.”

"I thought maybe one of his brain-trust friends might qualify as worthy." Kendall followed her comment with a raised eyebrow.

Now, Rachel looked confused. "My father wasn't a member."

"His file says he was," Bill confirmed. He took a minute to explain to Seth. "It was a group of professors you had to be invited to join, kind of the best of the best. A little elitist if you ask me."

Rachel shook her head. "The notification came he didn't get invited, and it was the one time I remember him ever losing his cool at home. He threw the living room mirror across the hall. It took my mother and I hours to find all the shards." She frowned. "In fact, the year before my mother died, one of my teachers suggested I might qualify in the future. He disappeared for two days afterwards."

The agents exchanged perplexed looks. Kendall spoke more slowly now. "It might mean nothing, but it seems strange no one ever figured it out. He told everyone, even his employers, he was a member of long standing."

Rachel offered a twisted smile. "Oh, I'm sure he told them a lot of lies. They just never asked for proof."

Bill sighed. "Our best guess at who might be inclined to copy him would be someone from that group or a student. I guess the information helps us narrow down the pool, at least." He scribbled another note. "Now, we just have to consider the thousands of male students who he taught." Taking a long swig of his beer, he leaned back. "I don't suppose he had a favorite student?"

"No one I remember," Rachel replied. "He mostly

referred to them as 'his little dweebs.' " She frowned. "It was kind of sad, because they worshipped him."

"They never figured out why all of his victims were blonde, either," Bill said. "Any theories?"

Rachel appeared surprised to be asked. She paused. "They made a big deal of the fact my mother and I were both brunettes, suggesting maybe a tiny part of him wanted us to be safe."

Bill looked doubtful. "How do you feel about their theory?"

"That it's bullshit." She tossed back the rest of her drink. "I'm pretty sure my father didn't give a damn about anybody but himself. They were just grasping at straws."

"I agree." Bill came to his feet, gesturing at Kendall. "Well, you gave us a few things to tug on. I appreciate your insight. We're going to interview your neighbors tomorrow."

A smile lightened Rachel's face. "You'll love Amos, and his wife will offer you cookies. Take them. They're worth the calories. Hobart—well, I wish you good luck with that asshole. He's a waste of good flesh."

Bill choked back a laugh as Kendall opened the door and they exited. Rachel leaned out and told the dogs to sit, which they did, looking at the other two people with curiosity. The dogs stayed as Seth and Rachel stood on the porch and watched the SUV exit the drive.

Chapter Sixteen

Opening the door, Rachel freed the dogs and they scrambled inside, butting Seth's legs with enthusiasm. "Settle down," she warned them and they looked up, chastised, not willing to jeopardize their dinners.

"They weren't so bad, right?" Seth said, interested in hearing her point of view.

She shrugged. "They weren't as intrusive as the last bunch were. Not yet, anyway."

"What did you think of Bill?"

"I think a lot of people underestimate him, which would be a big mistake."

He agreed. "I think she's the better front person and that frees him up to see the bigger picture. They work well together." His stomach rumbled, and he laughed. "So, what can I make us for dinner?"

"I have some of those pre-formed burgers we could grill, along with tomato and condiments. Sound okay?"

Seth nodded. "Does the grill on the back step work?"

"Yes." She pulled the meat patties out of the freezer, along with a package of buns. The dogs immediately started whining. "Oh, hell. I forgot to feed them."

"I'll do it." He picked up their bowls and headed for the appropriate cupboard. Reaching into the big plastic container, he pulled out the scoop. "Two each, right?"

"Yes." She watched him deliver the bowls to their normal spot. "You're very observant."

"Have to be in this business." Seth headed for the back of the house. "I'll turn on the grill to heat up and then come back for the patties." Close to setting, the sun peeked over the hills, so he switched on the light. A slight breeze underscored the chill in the air. It reminded him to grab his coat when he returned inside. Rachel watched him slide it on.

"Getting chilly?"

Seth nodded. "Might light a fire tonight." He picked up the meat and buns. "Got any cheese?"

She reached back into the refrigerator and withdrew a package of pre-sliced cheddar, zipping it open with a practiced hand. Following him out onto the porch, she wrapped her arms around herself, watching as he pried the patties apart. "How many do you want?"

"One is fine. Thanks."

He grunted. "You're really making me look like a hog, you know."

"Why, are you going to eat the rest?"

He looked up to see her smiling. "No, but they're a bit small, so I'll eat three."

"Whatever you want, but it's not a contest, you know."

"Sure, it is. And I win." He shut the cover and listened to the meat start to sizzle as the grill heated. "When I was sixteen, I ate ten fully-loaded burgers to win a prize at the county fair."

"That's disgusting," she replied.

He laughed. "It's what teenage boys do. I was trying to impress Alice Gates at the time."

"Did it work?"

"For about ten minutes." He sobered. "Then I barfed it all up, somewhere in the vicinity of her brand-new shoes."

Her laughter rang out, and he wondered at the pretty sound. *Have I ever heard her laugh?* It made him rather proud to have accomplished it.

She wandered back inside, and ten minutes or so later, the burgers were ready. Seth carried them in to find condiments in the center of the table, along with plates and beer for both of them. They dug in and didn't say much as they ate. After Rachel finished hers, she sat back with a sigh and watched him eat. "There's something extra tasty about food grilled outside."

He nodded and continued to eat. The phone rang as he finished number two. She glanced at the caller ID and answered it. From what she said, it appeared to be Amos, checking in. "Yes," Rachel said. "They were just asking a few questions and having a look around. They were pretty reasonable to deal with, so far, anyway. Okay, Amos. Thanks." She hung up.

"Just checking in?"

Rachel nodded. "He wanted to know if they're 'difficult characters,' as he put it." She smiled. "Those words are about as negative as his language gets. Wish I could say the same thing."

"I'd say you've handled things pretty well, thus far."

"Thanks." She started to clear the dishes as he took his last bite. "You make it easier than most." The compliment pleased him more than he should admit. He helped her rinse off the plates and slide them into the dishwasher.

"Do you want some dessert?"

"Lord, no," he said, rubbing his stomach. "Not tonight. I'm as stuffed as that old toy I saw Jack with."

Jack thumped his tail on the rug at the sound of his name. Both dogs watched and then lay their heads back down as Rachel and Seth settled in the den. In what was becoming a ritual, he found one comedy for them to watch and then another. At ten, he looked over and saw Rachel dozing. "I'll let the dogs out for a minute."

She murmured a sleepy assent.

He went to the door and let them out. They wandered, half asleep, down the steps, then, suddenly, Jack's head shot up. "Jack," Seth said, barely getting it out of his mouth before the dog shot away at warp speed into the darkness, a growling Zack not far behind. "Jack!" He felt Rachel rush up behind them and turned to reassure her he would go after them.

Seth heard the whine of a shot and threw himself at Rachel, yelling, "Down! Down!" They landed with a crash in the doorway, tangled around each other as he heard a second shot. This one was followed by a sickening screech, the defined sound of an animal in pain. He pulled the cellphone from his pocket, holding Rachel down with his other arm. Punching Wayne's number, he said "Shots fired. Notify the agents and approach with caution. Shots came from the Hobart side, on the hill. Hurry."

Seven or eight hellish minutes passed as he lay on the ground, holding a thrashing Rachel. "We have to help them," she cried, tears running down her face. She punched at him and he just held her tighter.

"Help is coming. We'll find them."

Moments later, the sound of a siren split the air and

it offered welcome reassurance. He stood up, crouching, waving Rachel to stay down. Peeking out the window, he saw the squad car barrel up to the house, followed by the SUV. They parked lengthwise to shelter the door. He eased it open to admit all three saviors. "No more shots. We think he shot at least one of the dogs." He forced himself to ignore Rachel's tear-stained face. "Wayne, stay with Rachel. She has a gun in the closet, top shelf, fully loaded, if you need it. We're going out. We'll warn you before we approach the house again."

"No," Rachel interjected.

He ignored her. "Does everyone have their flashlights?"

They nodded and inched out the door into the night. Whispering, Seth indicated the direction from which the shots originated, and they crossed the lawn. They split into individual units and worked through the whole section, using trees for cover when they could. Seth heard the dogs whining and made his way toward the sound. As he closed in, one of them started to growl, his eyes shining in the darkness. He spoke to reassure them. When they heard his voice, they settled. Seth sank to his knees on the grass beside the wounded one. It was Jack. He could tell by the broader shape of his head. As he inspected the wound, he heard a sound behind him and whipped around, gun aimed high. Bill stood there, lowering his pistol. "Is it bad?"

"Yes." Seth looked closer. "One in his hip. It's bleeding a lot." He twisted around. "Where's Kendall?"

She materialized out of the trees on the other side. "I think he's gone."

Seth cursed and peering through the thin beam of

light, called Wayne. "We're returning to the house. One of the dogs is hurt. Get Rachel ready, and we'll take him to see Doc Rivers. Call his emergency number as soon as I hang up, and tell him to meet us at the clinic."

Hanging up, he gestured to the other two. "Stay on either side of me, just in case. I'm going to carry him to the squad car. Rachel and I will take him to the vet."

"How about the other one?" Bill asked.

He murmured to reassure the dogs. "He'll follow." Holstering his gun, he handed his flashlight to Bill. Leaning down, he hoisted Jack into his arms. The dog cried out at the pain. "Sorry, pal. We're going to get you some help." At eighty pounds, the dog was hardly a lightweight but laid his head against Seth's chest as if he understood he shouldn't struggle.

As soon as they reached the cars, Rachel burst out the door with Wayne struggling to keep her inside. "Let her out," Seth said. The younger man obeyed, and she flung herself down the stairs. "Get in the squad car. I'm going to tilt the seat back and lay him on top of you, so you can support him."

"Doc will meet you there," Wayne offered.

Seth set Jack down on Rachel's lap, trying to help her support the large dog as best she could by belting them in. He closed her door. "Take Zack inside," he told Wayne. He pointed at the agents. "They're in charge until I get back." He threw himself into the driver's seat and started the engine. "Hold tight," he warned Rachel and threw the car into drive, splattering gravel as he turned to rocket down the slope. The only sounds he could hear were the thumping of his heart, Rachel's sobs, and the whimpering dog.

Seth made it there in six minutes flat, using the

siren only as a precaution to pass through three traffic lights. When they arrived, David Rivers stood in the open doorway, the light shining from behind him. The veterinarian urged them to a table and then waved them to one side. "Let me take a look." He pulled the bloody hair aside. "Any blood on the other side?"

"No. The bullet's still in there. I looked—no exit wound."

The vet nodded. "We need to remove it, but we have to stabilize him first. He's bleeding too much for surgery right now. The anesthesia might kill him."

"I can help," Seth offered.

He nodded, filling a syringe from a nearby bottle. "I'm going to give him something to make him comfortable. Just watch those teeth. Dogs in pain sometimes lash out."

"Got it." He watched as the vet injected Jack. He didn't respond much. *Is that good or bad?*

David worked in silence and the bleeding finally slowed, but Jack appeared less responsive. "It's okay. He needs some intravenous fluids to replace what he's lost." The vet took the bag of saline from Rachel and set up an IV, inserting a needle into a front leg and taping it down. After a double check, he stepped back, stripping the bloody gloves from his hands. "Seth, you can just let him lie all on the table now. He's down for the count."

They watched and waited for an anxious hour or more as the vet checked his vitals over and over. Finally, there was improvement as his heartbeat steadied.

"Okay. He's doing a little better now. It's safer if we limit the anesthesia and keep him semi-conscious.

Here we go," the vet said, reaching for the clippers, shaving away the hair to reveal the hole. He splashed some liquid around the wound, which made the dog jump. Seth tightened his hold. Jack cried out and Rachel moved to a spot near his head, crooning his name. It seemed to calm him, and the vet made an incision, then slid his fingers inside to feel around, half of his finger disappearing into the hole. "Where are you, you little bastard?" he whispered. He continued to probe. "There you are. Rachel, get ready with some of the big cotton square four by fours you see on your right. When I pull this bullet out, you get in there and stuff the gauze right in the hole and hold it tight, okay?"

She nodded, grabbing the wads of cotton and standing ready.

David reached in with forceps and pulled the bullet out, dropping it into a metal basin with a clang as Rachel pushed past him to do her job. The wad grew red almost instantly, and she looked up at the vet, panic contorting her face.

David grabbed some more pads, added them on top and applied more pressure. He showed her how to do it and then stepped back to get a needle and thread ready to stitch up.

Seth placed the bullet in an evidence bag as the vet made hurried stitches to close the gaping wound. "It may not be pretty, but it'll do."

"Is he okay?"

David sighed. "We've done all we can. He lost a lot of blood, but he's a young, healthy dog. A few inches closer to his abdomen and we would never have made it this far." He frowned. "Who in hell shot him?"

"We don't know."

He looked at Rachel. “Does this have anything to do with the problems at your place, Rachel?”

She nodded, teary again. “I think so.”

“I’m sorry for all your troubles. You don’t deserve it.”

She seemed surprised at his kindness. “Thank you.”

“We appreciate you comin’ in so fast, David,” Seth said.

The vet gave a tired smile. “No worries. The wife’s used to it after thirty years.”

“Can we stay here with him?” Rachel’s voice trembled with the words.

The other man nodded. “I’m going to hang some more saline to keep him going until I get back. You know how to change the bags, right Seth?”

“Yes. I’ve done it a time or two.”

“Good. Young Tommy will be here at six a.m. to feed breakfast and clean the kennels. I’ll text to warn him you’re here. I’m headed home for some sleep. Just make sure to lock up behind you if you decide to leave.” He headed toward the door. “You can pull those bucket chairs out of the waiting room. They’ll be more comfortable.”

“Thanks.” Seth watched through the front window as the lights from the vet’s car retreated. Rachel stood at Jack’s head, stroking it.

“I’m going to call Wayne and fill him in, then I’ll move those chairs in for us.”

She nodded.

Seth called and advised the other three with Wayne’s phone on speaker. “Get some sleep. We can’t do anything until daylight. Let’s meet back at the property at seven, and we'll see what we can find." He wondered, briefly, if the dog would be dead by sunup and pushed the thought away.

Chapter Seventeen

Dragging in two chairs from the front room, Seth pulled them right next to Jack. After that, he went and found the snack machine, hunting them up a drink and crackers each, along with two chocolate bars for energy. Rachel shoved them away, and he pushed them right back. "You won't do him any good if you get sick. He's going to need a lot of care for a while." He smothered his doubts the dog could survive, worried she might fall apart if he didn't.

Rachel stirred and began to stand. "Oh, no. How about Zack?"

He touched her arm. "Wayne took him to his house, for now. He has a real friendly old coon hound who will keep Zack company until we work this out."

"Thanks." She sat down again, laying her cheek against Jack's paw. "Why would that monster shoot a defenseless dog?"

Seth, touched by the emotion on her face, cleared his throat. "Either that was always his plan, to try and strip your protection away, or they came too close to catching him. Hard to tell which." He took a swig of his soda. "But he's having way too much fun, which means he'll get sloppy. And sloppy always works in our favor."

She remained quiet for a while, and then he noticed she had drifted off to sleep, her head lying on crossed arms. Seth put his jacket over her shoulders to guard against a chill. His mind wouldn't stop circling. All he could focus on was whether they would find anything in the woods when they could search. He spent the next few hours thinking through the case, wondering what they were missing. Suddenly, Jack whined.

Rachel woke at once. When she whispered the dog's name, patting his ears with a gentle hand, his tail thumped once on the table. It brought tears to her eyes, and he pretended not to notice. "He's a little stronger."

Seth heard tires on gravel and went to the front window, seeing Tommy, the kennel attendant, climb out of his truck. He went to meet the younger man and brought him back to check Jack. Tommy nodded to Rachel and then took a look. "Just leave him be, if he'll stay still. David should be in anytime now."

Seth and Rachel split one of the chocolate bars, encouraged when Jack raised his head to sniff at the treat. After about twenty minutes, they heard David pull up. He shoved the front door shut and came right in. "How's our poor boy doing?"

"He lifted his head and tried to wag his tail," Rachel told him, her expression hopeful.

The vet nodded, checking Jack's eyes and using a stethoscope to listen to his heart. "Reckon he looks better than we had any right to expect." He patted the dog's flank. "Rachel, you keep an eye on those teeth of his. I'll change his dressing and give him another shot for the pain. Then we can transfer him to a kennel, where he'll be more comfortable." She nodded and moved up to control his head. Although the bandages he stripped away were laden with blood, it was clear the wound had stopped seeping. The only objection from

Jack was a little whine.

When they had replaced the bandages with fresh ones, Doc stepped back and leaned out into the hall. “Are we all set, Tommy?” At the sound of assent, Doc turned to Seth. “Can you carry our tough guy to the back, Seth?”

Nodding, Seth waved Rachel away and slid his arms under the dog. “I gotcha, buddy,” he murmured, lifting the dog against him, letting his head fall against one shoulder. He followed the vet down a hall to a kennel area where a soft bed lay ready. Seth laid him down on his uninjured side, smiling when the dog thumped his tail once in gratitude.

“See if he’ll try to drink, Rachel.”

She pushed the bowl beside his head, and lifting it, he took a few laps of water. The mere sound of it proved reassuring.

Doc shook his head. “Young dogs can amaze us all. You take such good care of them, Rachel. It makes a difference. It really does.” He patted her on the back. “Leave him here with me for the day. We’ll push fluids and see how he does.”

She nodded. “Can I call you later?”

“Of course. You call me or come see him whenever you want.” He frowned. “Right now, both of you need a little shuteye. So, scoot.”

Seth knew there wouldn’t be much sleep for him today, but the sun was rising. Time to head to Rachel’s. They both climbed into the car, and he drove toward her place. At some point, he realized she was staring out the side window with tears travelling down her cheeks. He reached over, one handed, and gave her a clumsy pat on the arm. “He’s gonna be okay, Rachel.

He just needs some sleep and so do we."

She nodded, brushing her sleeve against her face. They made the rest of the drive in silence. Wayne and the others were parked in the lower pasture, standing outside and talking, their hands wrapped around mugs as they waited. Seth climbed out first.

"Morning," he offered.

Wayne spoke first. "How's the dog?"

"Made it through the night and he's stronger, now. Took a little drink. The vet thinks he'll be okay."

"Where's Zack?" Rachel asked. The dog must have heard her voice, because suddenly, there was a mournful face pressed against the window of Wayne's car. His nose poked through the crack of open window Wayne had left for air. She rushed to let him out and didn't notice Bill's hasty step back. The dog bounded off the seat, shoving against Rachel's legs, head raised for a pat. She dropped down and hugged him, managing a breathless chuckle when he licked her face.

"Why don't you take him up to the house and get some sleep? We're going to be busy for a while." Seth noted her grateful smile as she nodded.

After a few steps, she turned back. "Thank you for your help last night, all of you. I appreciate it." She headed up the hill.

Seth watched as she let herself in. Bill paused beside him. "I think those words are the most I've ever heard her say," he commented.

"She's had a hard life," Seth responded.

"It wasn't a criticism," Bill said. "If anything, I'm kind of surprised she's as normal as she is, given her circumstances." He set down the mug on the hood of their SUV and pulled on his gloves. "Now, where do you want to start?"

****

Rachel grabbed a shower while she could, talking to Zack as he lay next to the toilet. The poor guy didn't have a clue what to do without his brother around and had been restless since they came inside. He even picked at his breakfast.

She toweled off, thinking about Seth. He had to be exhausted, but he just kept going. His kindness last night hadn't been a surprise, but it felt strange to rely on someone, anyone, the way she did him. It gave her pause.

Pulling on fresh clothes, she brushed her hair and tailed it back, out of the way. Glancing out the window, she saw her saviors spread through the trees, searching. Eating a small bowl of cereal made her stomach settle, and she lay down on the couch, not knowing how long their search would take.

A while later, a soft knock woke her. She padded to the door, Zack behind her. Opening it revealed Kendall, who smiled. "We're done for now. Seth said to tell you he's going home to catch up on sleep. He'll be back later."

"Did you find anything?" Part of her knew the agent wouldn't be forthcoming, but she had to ask.

The other woman shrugged. "Nothing too exciting. We'll see what the day brings." With those empty words, she turned and left.

Rachel drank a glass of milk and lay down again, watching as Zack settled on the floor next to her. She trailed a hand on the top of his head. "He'll be home soon. Don't worry." The dog thumped a tail. "Your brother, I mean. Who did you think I was talking about?" Zack wiggled and lay his head down. She followed his example and slept.

****

Seth finished packaging up what they'd found to send to the lab. Would they get lucky enough to find DNA on the cigarette butt? Probably not, but it hadn't been there when they searched before, so it was worth a try. And the candy wrapper might be a wash, too, but they were desperate for a lead. Luckily, the agents could get it processed at their lab quicker than he ever could.

He had sent Jeb off with Wayne, so the two of them could patrol the town and take a few normal calls. He felt confident, trusting their youth and energy to cover the bases.

Rosie tucked her head in the door. "Time to get some sleep, boss. Your eyes are getting that glazed look."

"On my way." Seth handed her the evidence. "Kendall will be in for these soon. She and Bill are just grabbing breakfast." He shut the door behind himself. "I'll be home until five, then I'll drop in before I head to Rachel's."

She raised an eyebrow. "So, you plan to let the FBI agents fill in the press at two o'clock?"

"Oh, hell. I forgot all about the press conference." The mere idea of it made him grouchy.

"I'm sure they'd cover it if you asked them."

He shook his head. "They already have interviews scheduled for today."

Rosie looked surprised. "With who?"

"Amos and Hobart."

She smiled. "They'll receive the county's best

cookies from one and a substantial pain in the ass from the other."

"Yeah. I warned them." He glanced at his watch, noting how his sleep time had dwindled. "I can still catch a couple hours of rest and a shower. I'll be back by one thirty, then. Call me if you need me." It was an unnecessary reminder, but Rosie always tried to shelter him from annoyances when she could.

Seth yawned his way home, waving at a few neighbors on the way. Dragging himself out of the car took more energy than expected. He entered through the front door and starting pulling off clothes as he went, making it as far as his recliner. The too-quiet house gave him pause, then he slept.

The irritating peal of his phone alarm woke Seth at one p.m., and he glared at it with gritty eyes until remembering he still needed a shower. Sighing, he levered himself upright and dragged into the bathroom. The face greeting him in the mirror needed a shave. "Damn it," he muttered, digging in the drawer for shaving cream. He pitied women who had to worry about shaving their legs. Someone would have to pay him big bucks to waste time worrying about something so ridiculous.

After his shave, he raised the shower to a hellish hot temperature before he stepped in. It stung a little at first, then the heat pounded on his muscles and he felt them relax, one by one. Then Rachel's face filled his head. Oh, hell no, he couldn't allow the idea of that woman in the shower with him. It wasn't professional. It wasn't even smart. But he'd seen a different side of her now. Her strength inspired him, and her tenderness with her dog last night just about did him in. *And isn't that convenient?*

Nope. Not convenient. And neither was the way his body responded to hers last night, as they sat, side by side.

His mind riddled with coming conflicts, he leaned over and turned the temperature to cold.

Chapter Eighteen

Late in the afternoon, Rachel called the veterinarian, and his assistant told her Jack could come home as long as David could check on him the next day. He thought the dog would fret less at home and Rachel agreed. She called Seth. "I'll need your help with him. Should I just wait until you show up?"

"Actually, why don't you just pick me up here? We can stop by my place for fresh clothes and then go fetch him."

She thought about what people might think, and suddenly, didn't care. "Okay. What time?"

He paused. "Give me an hour. I can leave at five, and the clinic's open until six. We'll be at his place by five thirty."

Rachel paced around for forty-five minutes and then talked to Zack. "We're bringing him home, and everything will be okay again." He pushed his head against her knee, and she reached down to stroke him. Pulling out a nylon bone to keep him occupied for a while, she gave it to him and headed to the truck.

Seth and Rosie were leaving the building as she drove up. The other woman waved with a smile and climbed into an old sedan. Seth shook his head as she drove away, and he slid into Rachel's passenger seat. "Been telling her to have that carburetor cleaned for months."

"Maybe she can't afford to get it fixed," Rachel suggested.

He admitted, "I didn't even think about it. When this mess is over and done with, I can do it for her."

Rachel reversed and started to drive. "You've had a lot on your plate, mostly because of me."

Taking note she headed in the right direction at the fork, he asked, "Do you need directions?"

She shook her head. "Amos's wife told me where you live and all kinds of interesting things about you."

"Now, you have me worried."

Rachel smiled. "Edith thinks you're a fine young man, raised right and darn good lookin', too." She chuckled. "Thinks you should have been married years ago, since, according to her, you have your pick of the litter."

He groaned. "I love the folks in this town, but they've been trying to fix me up since I was about fourteen. Welcome to the south. If you don't have kids by the time you're twenty, you've missed the boat."

"At least you know they care."

"That's true." He was quiet for a few minutes, then they swung onto his street. "It's the third one on the left."

Rachel wasn't sure what she had expected, but the neat little ranch with the flowered border surprised her.

"It was my folks' place," he said, answering the unasked question.

"It's pretty," she answered as they came to a stop in the driveway. Although older, the house appeared very well maintained, making her wonder if Seth was handy, on top of his other skills.

He hopped out, slamming the door. "Come on in."

The inside reassured her he really did live here. He had what she thought of as the stereotypical bachelor setup: a large television, a music system, and both a leather recliner and couch. “Welcome to Man Land. I’ll just grab a few clothes, and we’ll be off.”

After he disappeared into another room, she wandered over to the bookcase. Not surprisingly, there were titles on murder and lots of mystery and suspense novels. But books on psychology and history were there, too, which showed her another, more academic side to him.

Interesting.

As she ran through the titles, he exited the back room, duffle bag in hand. “What do you think of fried chicken for dinner?”

“Only if you know how to cook it, because I don’t.” She didn’t feel like learning tonight, either.

He shook his head, in apparent pity. “I’m talking about Momma’s fried chicken.”

“The dumpy old place by the railroad tracks?”

He laughed. “The very same.” Gesturing for her to follow, he locked up behind them. “Babe Hankins, the aforementioned Momma, cooks the best fried chicken in the state. And better yet, biscuits made to melt in your mouth and cherry pie that makes you cry for your momma.”

She sighed. “I can see I’m going to gain ten pounds just hanging out with you.”

“Thought you didn’t like pie.”

“I don’t like peach pie. I love cherry. It’s not chocolate, but I can forgive that, if it’s as good as you claim.” He was almost too easy to be with, which made for dangerous territory, but for this one night, she would give herself permission to try and forget about everything. “Momma’s, it is.”

After the purchase, they stacked the food in the back of the truck and headed to pick up their patient. When they arrived at the vet’s, they were thrilled to see Jack standing up. The vet shook his head. “He’s doing surprisingly well, and he’s better off at home. No exercise at all for a while, just a little walk out to do his business. Absolutely no running for two weeks, at least.” He handed her a container of pain pills and went over the instructions. “Reduce his food by a third, since he won’t be getting his exercise. I’ll come by tomorrow, to make sure we’re still on the right track.”

Thanking him, Rachel paid the bill as Seth helped Jack into the truck. She steered around corners with care as Seth steadied him, but they managed fine. Jack became excited as they drove up the driveway, and Seth had to keep him from jumping down when he opened the door to exit, lowering him carefully instead. After entering the house, they watched the brothers greet each other with sniffs and happy mumbles. Seth returned to her truck for the food, shooing away the dogs when he arrived back inside with the aromatic bags.

She dished out the dog chow, watching to make sure Jack ate, while Seth removed plates from the cupboard. “Did you get any sleep?”

“A couple of hours,” he answered, opening the fridge to find drinks. After a pause, he put the beer back. “This will put me down for the count if I drink it tonight.”

“You’re going to need real sleep sooner or later. I’m not sure how you do it.”

Seth grinned. “Years of practice. In New York,

we'd go a week or so with almost no sleep when a hot case was running."

"Do you miss it?" Just because she didn't like city life didn't mean somebody did.

He shrugged. "I miss the brotherhood of it, I guess. Other than that, no. I don't miss all the people and the constant noise. I'm glad for the experience, but I never intended to stay." Gesturing toward the food he'd laid out, he waited while she helped herself to a piece of chicken, a side of coleslaw, and two biscuits. Loading up a plate twice the size of hers, he sat down in the opposite chair.

Rachel took a bite. The crispy outer layer gave way to juicy chicken heaven underneath. Chewing, she gave him the evil eye.

"Are you kidding? You don't like it?"

She swallowed. "I'm thinking I have more calories in my future, thanks to you."

"And you haven't even tried the biscuits or the pie," he added, pushing them her way. For a while, they ate in companionable silence.

Eventually, she shoved away from the table. "I'm saving my pie for later." She stood and started to gather their plates.

He joined her, surprising her by delaying the sweets as well. "If I don't, I might explode, and it won't be pretty."

She laughed and glanced at the dogs, who had retired to the den. Jack had fallen asleep against Zack, as if he needed the additional support. She and Seth settled in the chairs. "Did you guys find anything in the woods this morning? Kendall wouldn't tell me anything."

"Don't take it personally. They don't know you like I do." He cleared his throat. "We found a cigarette butt and a candy wrapper. The agents sent them to their lab, priority, so we should have something in a few days."

Rachel nodded. "The wrappers were a bust last time, but I guess you never know." Thinking for a moment made her remember. "How did the interviews with Amos and Hobart go?" She tried for a look of innocence, but the mere thought of the agents with Hobart made her grin.

Seth chuckled. "I can see you pretty much know how it went. Edith offered them cookies and asked them about city life. Visiting Hobart made quite the experience, I guess. They said the house smelled so bad, Bill could hardly force himself through the front door."

"Nothing new there." She grimaced. "I've never been in the house, but the man has the worst body odor in history."

"It's a shame." Seth sighed. "His parents were pretty decent folks, but he's always been a lazy ass."

"Did he offer his usual assessment of me?"

"Hmmm," Seth responded. "A rather colorful opinion, apparently. I'm not sure if it's his usual one or not."

She lowered her voice to Hobart's gruff tone. "Girl's gotta be a lesbian, you know. Ain't natural for a woman not to have a man in the house."

It made him laugh. "Good you have a sense of humor about it. He's not going to change anytime soon."

"As far as Hooky Hobart is concerned, I am a

lesbian."

He stared at her. "I won't tell him any different."

"How would you know about me?"

Suddenly, the air between them seemed to shift. He stretched out a foot from the kickstand of the recliner and tapped her foot. "I understand more than you think," he said, in an undertone.

The ringing of his phone dissected the moment, and with a sigh, he answered. Wayne's anxious babble proved loud enough for both to hear. Seth interrupted, "I'm on my way. Just keep everybody out until I get there." He hung up and turned to Rachel. "We have a domestic dispute. Can I borrow your truck?"

"Of course." She ran for the keys, thrusting them at him. "Nobody's hurt, I hope."

"No, but we've been there before and they can get pretty toxic. It's a little more than Wayne can handle by himself. I'll be back when I can."

"Of course."

Two hours later, Rachel gave herself a lecture. She had been pacing around the house since he left, fretting about his safety and trying to find something to do.

What the hell is happening to me?

She damned well knew better. Getting used to his company was a dangerous road for her to travel. Accustomed to being alone, she knew alone meant safe, and she had a lot of practice at it. So, why did his face float into her mind every time she closed her eyes?

Her phone rang and she grabbed it, despite her reservations. "Hello?"

"Hey, gorgeous," a voice purred. "How's your doggie friend? Is he sporting a few extra holes?"

The chilling words froze her for a moment. She

swallowed nausea and willed her hands not to shake. "Next time, it'll be my gun and your sorry ass, you coward."

The voice on the other end made tsk-tsk noises. "Is that any way to talk to your father?"

She put a hand to her heart and felt its speedy rhythm. "My father's dead, you asshole. You're just a pathetic wannabe."

"I'm the superior version, something you'll be certain of when I slice you up for the world to see," he bit out, the tone of his voice rising with each word. "He didn't claim you, but I will. Be ready, because not even your half-wit hero can save you." The last few words were almost a shriek, and then suddenly, she held a phone offering nothing, but dead air. Rachel turned it off, shaking, and stumbled forward, reaching for a pen and paper. The dogs clustered around her feet, reading the atmosphere. She grabbed for the puffer she'd purchased at the pharmacy and inhaled, then grabbed the pen and started to write down what the monster had said. Holding the implements, she sank down on the floor, scribbling as fast as she could.

Chapter Nineteen

A knock sounded and the dogs erupted in howls. Rachel ran for the closet, grabbing the gun with trembling hands. She sucked in a breath, and carrying the weapon down by her side, she inched to the door. "Seth?" she called, her voice too loud.

"Yup. Just me." Rachel peeked through the window to be certain and saw the sleeve of his coat and her truck parked back in its spot. Reassuring the dogs, she yanked open the door, ushering him in and slamming it shut behind him.

He stared at her, then at the gun in her hand, his concern evident. "What's wrong?"

"We're okay." She waved him to one of the kitchen chairs and walked over to take another puff of her inhaler. Grabbing the pad she'd written on, she sank into the opposite chair. "He called." She watched as the color washed out of his face and handed the pad to him.

He read it, slowly, then read it again. "Okay, let's talk impressions. First, are you sure it was a man?"

"Yes."

"Okay, now I know you can't be certain, but did you get an idea of his age?"

She thought about his choice of words and the arrogance. "Maybe late twenties? His voice sounded too mature to be a teenager, but he didn't have the control of an older man."

"That makes sense." He glanced back down at the pad. "Was there a change in his tone after you said the 'pathetic wannabe' part?"

"Yes. He lost control, then," she answered. "His voice became pretty shrill at the end." Reaching back, she pulled the band out of her hair, letting it spill around her shoulders. Maybe the release would keep her building headache at bay. She huffed in a breath, the air coming easier now. "I don't know if I made it worse. I didn't know what I should say."

His urge was to stroke her hair, but he leaned over and patted her hand, instead. "You know, most authorities would tell you to never engage with a threatening caller, but this might help us."

"How?"

"It will allow the agents to make a stronger profile. Specific word choices and sentence structure can tell them a lot." He shrugged. "Do you think you remembered it word for word?"

Rachel nodded. "Pretty close, at least. I have an excellent memory."

"I don't know much about it, but it will be interesting to hear their opinion, come morning." He glanced at his watch. "Why don't you get some sleep? It's past your bedtime."

"I never asked about your domestic call. Was everything okay?"

Nodding, he sat down to remove his boots. "Sent the wife to her sister's for a few days, and he's in the lockup until morning." He sighed. "Pretty much status quo for those two."

For the first time, she noted real fatigue in his face. "Do you need anything before bed?"

Another one of those awkward pauses occurred, then he chuckled. "Nah, I'm good. Goodnight, Rachel."

Knowing she couldn't sleep, Rachel murmured goodnight and went to her room. Changing into a nightie, she lay down, thinking whirlwind thoughts. Concern about her dogs mixed with memories from the phone call, and then there was Seth. What on earth should she do about Seth?

Part of her knew exactly what to do with Seth. She strangled that part down with the control born of years of practice.

She lay for at least an hour, waiting to hear the gentle snores she'd grown accustomed to after the past days. They didn't come. *Is he awake?* The question had no sooner crossed her mind when she heard him go to the refrigerator and pour himself a glass of something. Rising, she wandered out. "Can't sleep?"

"No, dammit. Want to watch a movie?"

"Sure." She walked over and switched on the lamp. The dogs blinked, looking confused, then settled back down. They were blocking the chairs, so she took the couch instead. Turning on the television, she scanned through the guide as he finished his drink.

"Want some pie?"

It felt like an alternate universe tonight. "Sure. Why not?"

He brought them each a big slice, cherries oozing, along with a glass of milk. They settled on *North by Northwest* for a movie, one of Rachel's favorites Seth had never seen. Chasing bad guys seemed like an appropriate theme for tonight. The dessert plates were stacked on the side table in short order, along with the empty glasses.

After a while, she noticed Seth had fallen silent and, looking over, saw his eyes had closed as he slumped farther down on the cushions. She didn't want to leave but thought she probably should. As if he could hear her thinking, his eyes opened a crack. "Why don't you just lie here with me and watch Cary Grant save the day? If we fall asleep, hey, bonus. If not, that's okay, too. We can just watch another movie."

She hesitated.

Seth propped his head up on one arm. "When I say 'lie,' it's what I mean. We'll both sleep better, I bet, but it's your call." His calm eyes reassured her.

Rachel nodded and watched as he lay the rest of the way down and scuttled back, making room for her. Lying down next to him, she turned to face the television. His strong arm came around her waist and she almost jumped at the heat he created from that simple contact. "You comfortable?"

"Yes." Well, yes and no, she felt like saying. Was it comfortable to be aroused and to pretend you weren't? He seemed calm to her, but she felt anything but calm. After a few minutes, she heard his breathing even out, and stifling the response of her own body, she followed him into sleep.

Early the next morning, the dogs barking woke them up. She had a "where the hell am I" sensation, then the feel of her back against Seth had her jumping up. He opened his eyes as she went to check the window. "I think they're just hungry," he mumbled.

Wayne's car pulled up to the step. "No, Wayne's here. What time is it?"

He sat up and ran a hand through his hair, grabbing his watch off the end table and then laughing. "Hell. It's seven thirty."

She didn't remember ever sleeping until this hour. Turning the television off, she scurried past him, closing the bedroom door and yanking on her clothes in a panic. The creak of the front door opening made her pause.

"Morning, you two," Seth's voice carried.

Curiosity had her re-entering the den as she shoved her shirttail into her jeans. Another man had joined Wayne. He was a little taller and much huskier with dark hair. "Good morning," she offered.

The two young men answered, "Ma'am," in unison, their politeness making her feel ancient.

Seth gestured to the man she didn't recognize. "Rachel, this is Jeb, our new hire. He's Wayne's cousin. He just graduated from the academy."

"Congratulations." She cleared her throat. "I'm afraid I'm adding significantly to your workload these days."

"It's our job, ma'am," Jeb answered, and she could read the pride on his face.

Seth smiled. "I'll be out in a second, boys." He closed the door behind them, stopping to pat the dogs. Moving around the room, he gathered up his things. "I'm hoping to get word from the lab today on the butt and the wrapper. I'll let you know if we find anything out."

"Thanks." She didn't know what else to say.

He grabbed his bag and gave her arm a pat as he passed in front of her. "That's the best sleep I've had for a while, so thanks." Opening the door, he turned back. "See you tonight."

"Yes." She watched as the door closed and ignored

the dogs as they milled around her feet in confusion. They were hardly the only ones knocked a little off-base. She suddenly caught on and realized they just needed to relieve themselves. She whisked the door open, and they sprinted out to the bushes, wandering back in a moment to give her an expectant look. Grabbing her coat and boots, she put them on while standing on the porch.

****

Seth glanced in the rearview mirror as he drove away, watching as Rachel laced on her boots. Smothering a grin, he remembered how she had vaulted off the couch when the dogs woke her. Well, he woke up happy. And she'd be pretty shocked to know just how much she'd cozied up against him during the night.

Life was peculiar, he thought, listening to the cousins' chatter. If anyone told him he'd look forward to seeing Rachel at the end of the day, he'd have laughed.

And been wrong.

By the time they arrived at the office, the agents were already there, looking sleepy. Seth had texted them there had been contact with the suspect, and clearly, they were curious. He waved them all back to the lunchroom, where everyone could sit. "The suspect called Rachel last night, when I was out on a domestic disturbance. Thank goodness, she had the presence of mind to write it all down." He read the words so they could all listen.

Bill shook his head. "She shouldn't have taunted him. He obviously intends for her to be the finale."

"The question is why?" Kendall said. "Does he think Rachel was part of her father's plans? Or is he improvising?"

The younger men were listening with rapt attention.

"Do we know if anyone visited him in prison?" Seth asked.

Kendall shuffled through her notes. "The usual female prison groupies and a few people from his legal team. That's about it." She took a sip of coffee. "Is Rachel sure it was a male?"

Seth nodded. "She said when he became angry, his voice rose, but she didn't see how it could be a woman." He consulted the sheet of paper. "He says, 'I'm the superior version.' A sense of arrogance is what always sinks these guys, right?"

Kendall nodded, then she grinned. "I kind of like the 'half-wit hero' reference, though."

Seth smiled as the others chuckled. "The best gift anyone can give you is to underestimate you." He leaned back in his chair. "He won't see me coming until it's too late." Remembering the agents' schedule yesterday, he asked "How did the interviews go?"

"Pretty much as you led us to expect," Kendall replied. "The farmer and his wife both seemed to care about Rachel and be frightened for her. And the Hobart guy, well, words fail me. I think he's too lazy to climb out of his chair, never mind murder someone." She sighed. "We'll spend today narrowing down the list of male students. We made some headway yesterday, but there's so many."

"Sounds good. My deputies can take care of the everyday routine calls while I go grab a shower and some fresh clothes. Maybe by the time I get back, that lab report will be in. If not, I'll go set up a recording system at Rachel's in case he calls again." Agreeing, they all stood and set off in their different directions.

As Seth drove toward his home, he reminded himself to ask Rachel if he could look at the trinkets her mother had left behind. Likely nothing there, but he wanted to try anything that might point them in a new direction.

After lunch and a staggering amount of paperwork, the lab results came in. He knew as soon as the agents barged into his office, they had something. Kendall handed him the sheet and said, "I guess we were all wrong."

He scanned the report and looked up, incredulous. "Hooky?" He shook his head. "Can't be."

Bill looked offended. "Lab work doesn't lie."

Seth sat back down, thinking. "I guess it's too far from his house for the trash to have just blown into such a protected position."

Kendall agreed.

"We need to bring him in for questioning." Seth came to his feet, frowning.

"At the very least," Bill said, sarcasm lacing his comment.

Seth removed his gun from the desk and snapped it into his holster. "We all know these results aren't near enough to make a case, but it gives us something to work with."

The agents decided to follow him in their own vehicle, which gave him a chance to call Rachel and tell her. The vet was just leaving, having checked on Jack's progress.

"There's no way it's Hooky," she said when he gave her the news.

Her confidence made him feel better. “I know, but we have to check it out.”

“Of course.”

“I think the evidence was planted, but if so, we have to figure out how the real suspect got access.”

“That man is drunk half the time. Anybody could come and go.”

After he hung up, her parting words echoed in his thoughts. He reminded himself to check whether Hooky kept his doors locked.

As they approached the house, Seth took note of the battered shutters hanging lopsided. Hooky would run this place into the ground and sell it for a pittance. A damn shame, he thought, and wondered what Hooky’s parents would have made of their beloved home now. They gathered by the front walk and single-filed to the door. The bell didn’t appear to be working, so Seth hammered on the door with his fist. There was no answer.

“Is that his pickup parked by the shed?” Kendall asked.

Seth nodded. “Let’s check the kitchen door out back.”

Moving to the rear, Seth saw the open door first. He put out a hand to stop their progress and pointed. All three drew their weapons and advanced. Seth rapped on the door. “Hooky? It’s Sheriff Talbot.”

They heard the muted drone of the television, but nothing more. He stuck his head inside, his gun preceding the rest of him and repeated his words, louder. No answer. As he advanced another step, he smelled it, the undeniable scent of death. “Ah, dammit,” he muttered under his breath. He pointed up the stairs and to Bill, who headed up to make sure no one waited to ambush them. Seth and Kendall advanced into the main floor, fanning in both directions to cover each other.

Chapter Twenty

Hooky lay sprawled by the door to the kitchen, blood congealed on and beside his head in a pool, a wooden baseball bat a few feet away. The massive wound would have killed him in seconds. As Seth stood observing, the two agents joined him. Bill leaned over and looked. “What, maybe yesterday afternoon?”

“When did you leave after the interview?”

“About eleven,” Kendall answered. “So, sometime late yesterday or very early this morning by the looks of things. He’s been there for a while.”

Sighing, he called the coroner and then Wayne. “You come up and give me a hand. Send Jeb to Rachel’s and make sure he’s wearing a vest. He’s on protection duty until I say otherwise.” Then he called Rachel and told her what had happened.

“That doesn’t make any sense.” She sounded as confused as he felt.

“I know. Listen, I’m sending Jeb to stay with you.”

“I’m fine.”

He huffed out a breath. “Just do as I ask, okay? This takes things to a whole new level.”

She agreed and hung up. He sent thanks to the skies for women who didn’t argue at times like this, figuring it might be a first for Rachel.

In the meantime, Bill had grabbed a crime scene kit, and Kendall started taking photographs. Seth walked around, checking all the angles. "Someone just waited inside the kitchen door. Hooky never had a chance."

Kendall agreed. "Did he have any money hidden away, anything he bragged about?"

Seth looked around, unable to hide his distaste. "I doubt it, but after we're done with the body, Wayne and I can do a thorough search."

They spent the afternoon, the four of them, digging for fruitless hours, finding nothing but mounds of filthy clothes, piles of beer cans and stack after stack of pornographic magazines, evidence of a pathetic life.

They locked the house and sealed everything with crime tape. By the time they left, it was after eight p.m. Seth had never felt so filthy. Thank goodness, he had clean clothes in his bag. After the agents departed, he phoned Rachel. "I'm heading to you. Do you mind if I use your shower? It'll save me a trip home."

"Of course not."

"How's Jeb doing?"

"He's an excellent guard," she said, and he could tell the deputy was within earshot.

"Tell him not to shoot me, then. I'm coming now."

He drove to her place, approaching slowly, so they could see him. Shaking off the fact that this was starting to feel like home, he climbed the steps. The dogs barked as Jeb opened the door, his gun held down at his side. "Good man," Seth said. "You run home, grab some food and some sleep. Wayne's doing the same thing. Tomorrow will be a marathon, so we all need to catch a few hours of rest when we can."

"Yes, sir." He paused. "And thank you for trusting me to guard Miss Mann."

"You're welcome, deputy. Just stay on the ball and wear your vest every day. Hear me?"

Jeb assented, took the keys for the squad car Seth handed him, and headed out. As Seth watched him leave, Rachel peeked out from the bedroom and he saw she was toweling her hair. She blushed and dropped her hands. "I thought I'd get out of your way, so the shower would be free."

He laughed. "That's probably a good idea. I smell like a cross between stale beer and week-old laundry." Not to mention corpses, he thought, but kept it to himself. Bending down to unlace his boots, he asked, "So, did Jeb do us proud?"

Sinking down on the kitchen chair, she smiled. "He was great. Made me feel a little old, though, with all his 'Yes, ma'ams.' "

"Me, too." He straightened and placed his boots by the door. "Well, you know what I mean. I'm not really the 'sir' type."

"Shower first, then eat?"

"Yes. I'm starving, but a few more minutes won't kill me." He found his way into the bathroom and smelled girl soap or shampoo as soon as he entered. Even in his exhausted state, it aroused him, just because it was hers. She had laid out a big, fluffy towel on the counter with a fresh bar of more generic soap sitting on top.

The hot shower felt like heaven, and he used the soap to wash his hair. He could have stolen some of her shampoo, but smelling like flowers might damage his manly reputation. Glancing around her room as he dressed, he saw little more than an old Bible, a small jewelry box, and a few books. He liked the bed, though;

instead of some feminine contraption, a custom rustic build, sturdy and comfortable. Probably not a great idea to focus on the bed, but he was old enough to appreciate comfort. That's what he told himself, anyway.

Seth opened the door as he finished buttoning his shirt. Two thick, roast beef sandwiches waited at what now seemed like his regular place at the table. Rachel appeared out of the den, leaning into the refrigerator to grab him a beer.

"Better make it milk tonight if you have any left. Things are heating up. I don't want to get caught flat-footed."

She swapped it out and poured him a glass, handing it over. "I want to ask you one question and then let's drop it for the rest of the night."

"Sure." He took a bite.

"Are you certain it's the same guy?"

He shrugged, continuing to chew, then swallowed. "It's a bit of a stretch to think we have two killers in this town at the same time."

"True."

"Have you eaten?"

She nodded. "Jeb, the dogs, and I ate hours ago."

"They hardly moved when I came in." He saw them snoring against the sofa.

Rachel laughed. "Jack had to stay beside us, but Jeb and I took turns throwing the ball for Zack. He finally gave up, which never happens. Jeb has a pretty strong throwing arm."

"What do you think of him?"

"He's a Wayne clone, which is a good thing, of course. He's very serious about his career and pretty mature for his age. I think he'll work out great."

Since her opinion matched his assessment, he found her confirmation encouraging. He ate in silence, grateful the food tamed the hunger growls. He sat back, rubbing his stomach. “Thanks for the grub.”

“You’re welcome. Let’s watch a show for a while. I’ll bet you’ll be asleep in a shake.”

He nodded, stopping to set the alarm on his watch, then leaving it on the end table. As if it were second nature now, they both maneuvered around the dogs to sit on the sofa. Settling in, they switched on the television.

****

Ten minutes later, he fell asleep. He slumped her way, and all she could think of was how good he smelled. She’d had two lovers in her life, little more than space keepers to fill a sexual void. Wanting to feel like a normal person had been her primary incentive. It had proved minimally successful, for the short term at least. Could Seth be different? And would he ever want to be the lover of a woman whose only heritage was horror?

Rachel shoved the thought away and rose to her feet, realizing the way he lay left no room on the couch for her. Disappointed, she pushed a pillow under his head and covered him with the throw. A little distance might be a good thing. She crept into her bedroom, listening as the dogs mumbled in their sleep at the intrusion of her steps.

Eventually, she drifted off, but troubled dreams woke her a short time later to find a tall man standing in the doorway. Half awake, she pushed herself up on one arm, opening her mouth to scream.

“It’s Seth,” he said, at the same time she realized it

was him. "Are you okay?"

She let out an embarrassed sigh when she saw the gun he held at his side. "Crazy dreams. I'm so sorry I woke you."

"Sokay." Turning on the tiny lamp she kept in the corner, he rubbed his eyes and set his pistol down. He came to sit on the edge of her bed. The dogs appeared in the doorway. "It's okay, guys. Go lie down." Jack yawned, and they both disappeared around the corner.

Rachel looked up at him.

"Do you need something to help you sleep?"

His question hung in the air between them. She found she couldn't answer. Maybe he just meant a cup of cocoa. This was unfamiliar land, and there were many minefields to navigate.

"You and I, we're practical people. Right?"

Rachel nodded.

"I'll protect you with my life, no matter what happens between us." He took her hand and stroked the back of it. "But for both of our sakes, you need to spell out for me exactly what you want."

She trembled, and he raised her hand to his lips, kissing where he had stroked. "Do you want what we shared last night, or do you want more?"

This time, there was no hesitation. Just like that, she knew. "I want more."

He nodded and stood, leaning over to push the door shut. Turning to face her, he stripped off his T-shirt. She struggled not to gasp. His broad shoulders looked a yard wide in the dim light. He had those firm, smooth kind of muscles, not the overblown kind you see on gym rats. She couldn't look away, then he began to unbuckle his belt, and she pointed to the light.

“Leave it on,” he suggested. He slid off his jeans and shorts in one quick motion, and before she could blink, he was lying next to her, all heat and touchable skin. She gestured to her nightie.

“We’ve got time. No need to rush.” He propped up on one elbow and leaned in to kiss her. She’d never been much one for kissing, but she fell prey to this one. It started slow, like a tender fire, and built until she felt engulfed by the flames. Her hands roamed his shoulders, his back, unable to touch enough of him. When his lips moved to her neck, she pushed her clothing aside for better contact. She felt the chuckle rumble in his throat. “Do you want it off?”

She nodded.

“Say it.”

“I want it off.” Her words sounded strangled, but they were enough. His fingers worked down to the hem and raised it so slowly, she wondered if he tormented her on purpose. She ducked her head through, slid her arms out, and he tossed it out of the bed, onto the floor.

The sensation of her skin against his was almost too much to bear. He pushed back to look her over, head to toe. “You’re beautiful.” His fingers trailed down to brush her breasts, and she returned the gesture, combing through the hair on his chest. He bent to kiss her again. After the kiss, she let her teeth graze his neck and felt his answering shudder. He reversed their positions so she lay on top of him. Now their whole bodies were in contact, and the ravenous hunger that instantly doubled shocked her.

She could feel his heart hammering against hers and experienced rampant relief when she realized she wasn’t alone in this burning world of desire.

"Rachel?" He growled her name, and she answered by touching him, everywhere, and feeling his answering pulse. He reversed their positions, and his seeking fingers found her. "Say my name."

"Seth." She stroked the side of his face. He responded by whispering her name again as he eased inside her, taking his time, his eyes staring into hers.

It felt so right, she didn't know whether to laugh or cry. The intensity threatened to overwhelm her. She moved against him, seeking more, and he answered with an increase in rhythm. At some point, she realized with sudden clarity those helpless sounds of abandonment came from her.

And Rachel didn't care. She surrendered first, surging against him and feeling his strong hands bracing her. He followed her into climax, his breath rushing in and out, muscles straining. Afterwards, he moved beside her, one arm wrapped around her, the other reaching over to stroke hers. He inhaled, the breath coming out in a huff. "Is holy smokes too adolescent a comment at this point?"

She managed enough air for a one-word answer. "No."

"You okay?" He looked at her with concern. "Do you need your inhaler?"

Rachel shook her head. "I'm more than okay." She smiled, feeling like all the bones had been removed from her body.

He dropped a kiss on her forehead. "Life is always surprising, isn't it?"

Rachel snuggled deeper into his embrace. "That's an understatement," she murmured. It was the last thing she remembered before drifting off to sleep.

Chapter Twenty-One

Morning came too early, as it often does. Her alarm clock rang, and although they ignored it, the dogs didn't. Rachel heard their whines at the door. Rising to let them in, she almost laughed at their confused expressions. She grabbed her robe.

"Where are you going? Get back here."

Tying the belt, she turned to look at him, all tousled and impatient. "The dogs need to go out, and the boys will be here in thirty minutes. You have to get into the shower."

He grumbled and it made her chuckle. *Clearly not a morning person*. She walked to the door, peered out to make sure nothing lurked behind it, then let the dogs out. As they took care of business, she tried to remember when she had ever felt this good.

Never.

It didn't take away their problems, but it made them easier to bear. Whistling made the dogs return, and she closed the door behind them. She heard the shower running and leaned in to make sure he had everything he needed.

"Lots of room in here for two," he suggested, sounding more awake. "I texted Wayne and said they could have another thirty minutes to grab some breakfast."

She smiled, slipping off her robe. The world and all

its complications could wait another thirty minutes.

Afterwards, she made him coffee, putting it in a travel mug so he could take it with him. It was strange, thinking about someone else's needs, not just the dogs. "Want some cereal?" she called, turning to see him emerge from the bedroom.

"I can make some toast."

She shook her head, pointing to the clock on the microwave. "They'll be here soon, and you still have to pack your bag and get your boots on."

"Damn clock just keeps ticking." He grabbed his bag and packed it with his clothes from last night. By the time he had it filled and his boots on, she had the toast ready and waiting. He stood at the counter and ate it. "Wish it could be me staying here today, instead of Jeb."

"Me, too." Something between them had changed. She would figure out the parameters of that later.

Seth took a swig of the coffee. "He's bringing you a small recorder from the office. Anytime you answer the phone, put it on speaker, and lay the recorder as close as possible."

Rachel nodded. "What are you working on today?"

"I have a meeting with the town council and a press conference, too." He grimaced. "And won't it be fun, what with Hooky and everything."

"Is there anything I can do to help?" She felt useless, sitting around half the day.

"Sure." He leaned over and kissed her as she heard an approaching car. The dogs began to bark. "You and Jeb keep looking over the victim profiles. Never know when something will pop." He stopped on his way to the door to reassure the pups and opened it to find Jeb climbing the stairs. Wayne vacated the driver's position, waved to Rachel, and took the front passenger seat.

At the last minute, Seth paused. "Rachel, do you think you could show Jeb the things your mother left you? I doubt there's anything to discover, but you never know." Turning to Jeb, he added, "Sometimes instincts help. You think of anything relevant, call me."

"Yes, sir."

"And Jeb?"

"Yes, sir."

"When it's just us, you can call me Seth. When we're working with other folks, call me sheriff."

"Yes, sir…Sheriff."

****

As they drove away, Seth smiled, trying to remember being as young as Jeb. It wasn't hard smiling this morning.

"Seth, do you mind if I ask how my cousin is doing?" Wayne looked embarrassed about his question.

"So far, just great. Has he said much about it to you?"

The younger man laughed. "Can't stop talking about it. He'd work all day and all night if you let him."

"With the way things are going, that's good to know, but we all get sloppy with no sleep."

"True," he said. "You look like you finally caught up last night." He looked horrified at his own suggestive words and started to stammer.

"Calm down, Wayne. Yes, thanks, I got some sleep. I gather you caught up on yours after our call last night?"

He nodded with vigor. "Absolutely," he said. "And

I like her. Rachel, I mean. I know she mostly keeps to herself, but she's kind and smart."

"Kind and smart is more than we can say for some folks, right, Wayne?"

"Yes, Seth."

Quiet reigned for a few moments, then Wayne said, "Jeb wants to get married before he turns thirty, you know, and have kids as soon as possible."

"How about that." He tried not to smile at the incredulous tone in the deputy's voice.

Wayne shrugged, running a hand through his hair. "I guess I just don't get it. I mean, the town's full of pretty girls, right? Why limit yourself to just one?"

Seth smiled as they pulled into the station. "Believe it or not, that gets old after a while."

He sent Wayne off for the morning check in at the school. Inside, he found the agents already working on the never-ending list of college students. "Making any progress?"

Kendall nodded. "Down to twenty-eight. We should have it down to a short list by nightfall. They gave us a few new academy graduates to help us out on the legwork end."

He told them he'd be in and out all day, thanks to the meeting and other commitments. "Do you think you could join me for a news briefing at two this afternoon?"

"Mostly about Hobart?"

"I'm going to try and restrict it to him. I think we'll admit they're connected. They'll ridicule us if we don't."

Bill offered a grimace. "Damn press."

"In the meantime, I have a town council meeting. I

suspect they just want an update on all this, so I shouldn't be long."

"Better you than me," Kendall called after him as he left the room.

Within ten minutes, he wished he'd damn well opted out of the meeting. "No offense, Mayor Bradshaw. We are making important progress on this case, but having to attend extra meetings doesn't help."

The mayor kept fiddling with his cuffs and avoiding his gaze. "Seth, I know your intentions are above reproach, but it has been suggested that perhaps you aren't looking closely enough at Rachel Mann for these murders."

Seth sincerely hoped no one could see how angry the comment made him. He prided himself on his self-control. "Do you folks seriously think Rachel Mann shot her own dog?" Glancing around the seven people at the table, he could only see one other who didn't look sympathetic. "How many of us would like to be judged on the conduct of every person in our family?"

The single council member who seemed to side with the mayor stood, her nose firmly planted in the air. "I wonder about your conduct, Sheriff," she said, following the words with an indignant sniff.

"Do you want to clarify your comment, ma'am?" His momma would have been proud of the politeness which positively oozed from him.

She shot him a smug look. "I've seen your car at that woman's house at all hours of the day and night."

"And I'd be at your house at all hours of the night if you needed me, Mrs. Chastain." His statement earned a nervous chuckle from someone. "Either myself, a deputy, or an agent has been with Miss Mann frequently since this began, for her own protection. We trade cars all the time for the sake of preserving our budget, so it might be me or one of my deputies you saw. In order to address your concerns, I'll tell you Rachel Mann had a protective escort at the time of Hooky's death." He mentally crossed his fingers the official time of death would confirm his words. For now, he just relied on his experience with corpses.

Seth gathered up his notes. "I'm afraid I have to run. I have a press conference any time now." Nodding goodbye, he strode out the door before anyone could delay him.

Driving back, he tried to find something positive to dwell on. At least it had only been the mayor and Mrs. Chastain who were negative about Rachel. Chastain was the self-appointed social secretary of the town, and he was sure Rachel would never fit into the narrow definition she likely had for "acceptable."

It made him like Rachel even more.

When he entered the precinct, Rosie looked up from the computer. "Call Jeb when you get a moment."

"What's wrong?" The words came out in a rush.

She leaned over and patted his arm. "She's fine. Jeb said he found something you might think is worth a look. He doesn't want to talk in front of Rachel, though, until he runs it past you."

He glanced at his watch. "I have some time before the press arrives. Call and tell him I'll drop by." Before she could answer, he was backing up to head out. It only took a few minutes to get there. The dogs were outside with Jeb watching as he approached. Parking, he climbed out of the squad car. "Everything okay?"

"Yes, Seth. I hope I'm not wasting your time with

this."

"Don't worry. We need everyone's brain working on this thing." He reached down to pat the excited dogs. "What did you find?"

"There's two photographs in the Bible. Rachel said one is her momma and the other is a family friend who passed away."

"Got it." He heard a clock ticking in his head, but stifled it.

"The friend's name was Peter Smythe; he was British. He, Rachel's mom, and her father were close friends." As if sensing Seth's impatience, he sped up. "Anyway, here's the thing. He looks a lot like Rachel."

Seth struggled not to let doubt show in his expression. "What did Rachel say about him?"

"She said she never knew him. He died in a car accident, months before she was born." Jeb lifted his chin. "Seth, I know it's out of left field, but I'm really good with faces. And there's something else."

"Let's take the dogs in. We can talk about this in front of Rachel, and she'll be wondering what we're up to. Just don't mention the whole resemblance thing for now." He knocked as he entered.

Rachel was leaning against the counter, suspicion pursing her lips. "So, what's the big secret?"

"Don't worry. Jeb just has an idea." Seth looked and saw the items were spread on the coffee table in the den, including the little trinket box. "Let's sit and have a peek."

As soon as they took seats, Jeb picked up a photo and handed it to him. Seth leaned toward the lamp to see a little better. The man was tall and slender with blond hair and a ready smile. As he craned to look closer, Jeb handed him a magnifying glass. The shape of his head, nose, and ears was similar to Rachel. Was that enough?

Jeb took the photo out of his hand and replaced it with a ring. It had a school insignia on it. He was just about to say, "So?" when he saw an inscription inside the band. Using the glass, he read it: To darling R, Love P.

He looked up, and Jeb answered the unspoken question. "Her mother's name was Renee."

"Somebody needs to tell me what's going on, right now." Rachel spit the words out through clenched teeth.

"Did your mother ever tell you anything about the car accident that killed Peter?" Seth asked.

She played her fingers on the arm of the sofa. "I guess there was some big investigation, but then they just closed the case. Why?"

"I know he was friends with your mother and father, but did you get the sense he and your mother were close?"

Rachel closed her eyes. "She'd get really teary when she talked about him. And she said never to show anyone else the picture." Now, her eyes opened, blazing with understanding. "I guess she meant my father. I never really thought about it. We had lots of secrets." Leaning over, she grabbed Seth's arm. "What does it mean?"

"I'm not sure, but I think we need to look more into his life and the accident. Is it okay if I take the photograph with me? I'll make sure you get it back."

"Of course. Anything that might help."

Looking at his watch, he swore. "Gotta run. The damn press conference is in fifteen minutes, and I need to get Kendall working on this." He slapped Jeb on the back as he passed on his way to the door. "Good work, young man."

"Thank you, Sheriff," the deputy responded, pride lighting his face. Seth shut the door and made a beeline for the car. He just had enough time to explain everything to the agents before they came to stand beside him as he spoke to the press. With this latest death, the crowd of news people had doubled. He gave the update on Hooky's death and opened it for questions. Then came the inevitable question, "Is Rachel Mann a suspect in these killings?"

"No," he answered. "Miss Mann has been assisting in the investigation and had a protective detail with her when Hobart was killed." Thanks goodness, the timing had been affirmed in his absence.

The ferret-faced newsman was back. "Who is included in Miss Mann's detail?" His smirk said he knew exactly who was normally with Rachel.

"We have all served in that capacity in the recent past and will continue to do so. That's all the questions for today."

Seth went inside, and Rosie came to stand beside him, watching through the window as the crowd dispersed. "Not too bad today, considering they're bloodsuckers."

He laughed and told her about Jeb's idea. "For heaven's sake," she said. "He's taking the place by storm. Do you think there's really something to it?"

Shrugging, he headed down the hall. "We'll give it to the agents and let them figure out where it might lead." He found Kendall and Bill sprawled in their makeshift office, enjoying a late-afternoon break.

Handing them the photograph of Peter, he explained.

"Is it worth spending time on this when we're so short-handed?" Kendall asked. "I'm impressed he caught it, but—"

Seth and Bill both replied, "Yes," at the same moment. Seth indicated Bill should explain. "It might go to Dark Mark's motivation and therefore be connected to this guy in some way."

She nodded. "Okay. That makes sense. Do you want to take it, Bill, and I'll just keep on with the list?"

Her partner nodded, heading straight for the computer. Seth turned to Kendall. "How is the list?"

She rubbed her eyes, taking another sip of coffee. "We have five left, all with strong potential. We are working on full profiles for all of them."

"Any jump out at you as being your best bet?"

She smiled. "Bill says one of their photos gives him a hinky feeling. Not sure that will hold up in court."

"What happened last time I had a hinky feeling?" Bill asked, his gaze still focused on his computer.

Kendall rolled her eyes. "It's true. The young woman everyone else thought was a sweetheart ended up to be the culprit. No, Bill figures he has powers the rest of us mere mortals should envy." She laughed. "Anyway, this guy's name is Carson Gale. Might as well start with him."

"Hey," Seth replied, "I'll take any superpowers you can offer at this stage. Right now, I have a few stops to make in town, then I'll grab fresh clothes and head to Rachel's." Saying goodnight to everyone, he headed out.

Chapter Twenty-Two

Rachel had to smile at Jeb as he guarded her the way one might guard the president. He never left her side, his eyes scanning left and right, ready to vault on anyone who looked suspicious.

It was just the grocery store, for heaven's sake, not a celebrity appearance. She worked her way down the list. Having Seth and Jeb around meant having a lot more food available, but their presence still made for pretty cheap security. They were just finishing when her cart ended up impeded by a woman she didn't recognize. Before she could say anything, Jeb said, "Ma'am, could you please move your cart so we can get by?"

The other woman ignored him, addressing Rachel instead. "Haven't you caused enough trouble in this town?"

It stunned Rachel, but she recovered quickly. "I haven't caused any trouble. Excuse us, please." When the aggressor didn't respond with anything but a glare, Jeb moved forward. He showed his badge. "Clear the aisle, ma'am." He grasped the edge of the other woman's cart, moving it aside as the other woman tried to keep it in place. He placed himself between the troublemaker and Rachel, letting the latter slide past and then following her to the cashier. As Rachel started placing her items on the belt, the other woman raised her voice and it carried. "Polluted blood always tells, young lady. You might fool other simpletons like this young man, but you'll never fool the rest of us." With that, she turned and marched away.

Rachel felt ill.

"Don't listen to her," Jeb said in a whisper, as the clerk bagged the groceries. "She's an itch with a B. Always has been." The clerk apologized, too, looking appalled. But the nagging worry stayed with Rachel, and she wondered if the future would be like this if she stayed.

****

When Seth arrived at Rachel's, he found Jeb in the den with the dogs, looking tense. The younger man told him about what had happened at the grocery store with Mrs. Chastain.

"Well, damn. She caused problems at the town council, too." Seth sighed. "Thanks for telling me. How long has Rachel been in her room?"

"Since we got back," Jeb replied. "I just let her be, because I knew you'd be along pretty quick."

"Okay. Thanks for telling me. I'll talk to her." He saw Jeb out, touched by his concern. He didn't wait for inspiration, simply knocking on her bedroom door and letting himself in. She was laying on the bed, staring at the ceiling. "Are you okay?"

Rachel turned toward him, her tear-stained face testimony to her mood. "Not really."

"Mrs. Chastain has nothing to occupy her time but looking down at her neighbors. It's her full-time occupation." He sat down on the edge of the bed. "You can't let people like her get inside of your head."

"She has a point, though. Sooner or later, blood

will tell." Rachel rubbed her eyes with both fists. "He's always going to be my father. What if genetics has a time bomb in store for me?"

"I don't understand," he said.

Her voice shook. "There's no point to this, don't you see? I can never have a normal life with a husband and children. They might turn out to be like him. Hell, I might turn out to be like him."

"That's never going to happen."

"You can't know for certain."

He grasped her arms, staring into her eyes. "Yes, I do know. Both my heart and my head know, Rachel."

"I can't take the chance. I would never forgive myself." She scrambled out of the bed into the bathroom, slamming the door shut behind her.

He flaked out on the couch, talking to the dogs who collapsed beside it. He could hear her crying but knew she needed some space. *What the hell can I say to convince her?*

Thoughts of his own parents came to mind. They had been married forty-five years when a car accident claimed them both. He wanted what they'd had—a close, happy relationship. They had held hands until their dying day. Shoot, the old man had still patted his mum on the butt most every time he passed by, which had scandalized and embarrassed Seth as a teenager. Smiling, his mom used to say Seth would know when he met his mate. Back then, he had thought it was a bunch of nonsense.

Well, hell, maybe not. But what was a man supposed to do when the woman he wanted didn't believe in a shared fate. With a sigh of frustration, he drifted off to sleep.

Sometime during the night, he was awoken by the dogs grumbling in their sleep. He cracked open his eyes as he shushed them. Rachel stood two feet away, the dim light from the porch window gleaming off her naked body. He opened his mouth to speak, but she beat him to it.

"This is just sex."

"Rachel…."

"Be quiet." She nudged him until he lay flat on his back and then she climbed on top of him. Rubbing her body against his, every part of him sprang to life, never questioning. "This is what I need tonight."

"Okay." Like he would ever say no to her, could ever say no. Reaching up, he touched wherever his fingers reached; the slope of her breast, her thigh. Her hands scorched every part of him, then she moved, taking him inside her in one hungry jump.

Seth thought his overwhelmed heart might stop, the sensation of being surrounded by her so intense he could scarcely breathe. They surged together, her knees on either side of his hips, clasping. He held her tight and they moved together in immeasurable heat, her body silhouetted by the faint light. As if still in a dream, he said her name, breathless, and her helpless moans answered him. She refused to slow the frantic pace until, arching her back, she tightened and cried out. He held her hips snug against him until her body eased, then he abandoned all control and allowed himself the straining pleasure of release.

Afterwards, she lay slumped against him, and he stroked her back. His one thought was the certainty Rachel could never deny this connection, try as she might. When she tried to talk, through tears, he wrapped his arms around her. “Shhh…it’s going to be all right. We’ll figure it out when this nightmare is over.” After a few minutes, she gave in and her breathing calmed. When she finally fell asleep, he followed her.

In the morning, she had disappeared back into her room. When it came close to the deputies’ arrival time and she still hadn’t come out, he stuck his head in through the open doorway. She was lying, looking exhausted, staring at the ceiling. “Rachel.”

She turned her head to look in his direction.

“I never found the opportunity to tell you we have the potentials down to five people. Our number one suspect is a guy named Carson Gale. Ever heard of him?”

“No.”

He took two steps closer. “We’re making progress. You need to keep the faith.”

“Sure.” There was no conviction in the word.

Seth leaned over and kissed her cheek, feeling the dampness left by tears. “You don’t let one hateful old woman change your destiny, Rachel. That’s not who you are.” He felt her eyes on him as he headed for the door. “We’ll talk more about this later, when you’ve had a chance to get some sleep.”

****

Rachel thought about Seth’s parting words long after he left. She felt so tired, as if she’d never feel vital again. Her memory of last night gave her pause. For good or bad, such behavior was so unlike her. Needing someone, both sexually and emotionally, proved to be scary for her. It made her vulnerable, and wasn’t vulnerable the opposite of strong?

Dragging herself out of bed, she gave herself a mental kick in the butt. She had all of these people helping her. Now might be the time to help herself. She headed into the shower, hoping it might revive her.

An hour later, after showering, dressing, and having breakfast, Rachel felt almost human. She always tended to tackle too many things at once. Maybe now, she should try for one thing at a time. She spent until the early afternoon catching up on housework.

"Well, damn. We forgot the new bag of dog food in the truck." Rachel started toward the back door. "Lucky it didn't rain last night."

Jeb moved to intercept. "Let me get it, Rachel. The dogs have to go out, anyway."

"Okay. Thanks," she said, thinking about the lunch they hadn't eaten yet, even though it was almost two o'clock. "The bags are in the bed, by the toolbox." She realized after she said it Jeb already knew because he had placed them there. *I need more sleep, to get my brain back in place.*

Rachel started making sandwiches, her mind going back to Seth. She felt so confused. This situation defined frustration. She shouldn't be with him, but couldn't stay away as last night had proven. Seth was pretty much for the poster boy for the whole happily ever after scene. He deserved the whole picture, complete with white picket fence. She just didn't have enough to offer him.

As she finished preparing their lunch, the dogs started barking, and she realized, suddenly, Jeb was taking too long. *I'm just paranoid. The dogs are probably just chasing a squirrel.* Putting the food on the table, she headed toward the window to check. The only warning she had was a subtle change of shadows as the door whipped open before an arm wrapped tight around her neck and a man yanked her against his body. "Hello, daughter." He kicked the door shut.

Rachel squirmed and fought, reaching back to try and gain a hold. Then she felt the cold muzzle of a gun against her cheek and stilled. She took a deep breath. "Carson Gale, I presume."

"Bitch."

She had hoped her knowledge of his name would make him sloppy, but no dice.

He tightened his hold. "You think you're so smart."

"I am smart. Smarter than my father could ever be." She had to rattle him, somehow, had to find an opening to make a run for it.

"Excuse me for stating the obvious, but you're not looking too brilliant at the moment. You'd better watch it or I'll just dump your body like I did your deputy friend."

Ghastly pictures filled her mind. "What have you done with him?" She could hear one of the dogs barking from a distance.

"Well, the deputy's down for the count." The smirk in his voice frightened her as much as his words did. "It took five bullets to do it, so I'm rather impressed. In the end, all those muscles didn't help him much, did they?"

She closed her eyes, remembering Jeb wore a vest and praying it was enough to save him.

Carson shifted and started moving them both to the door in an awkward shuffle. "You better hope the dogs are obedient. Because you're going to make them lie down, and if you don't, I'll shoot them. And I've already proven I can do it." He shoved her against the door, so the knob hit her stomach. "You're going to open the door slowly. When the dogs approach, you tell them to lie down. And then we're going for a ride, Rachel. It's time for us to make history."

As soon as the door cracked open, both dogs ran to the base of the stairs, barking and growling, the hair on their backs ridging up. "It's okay," she coaxed, trying to inject some calm into her voice. "Lie down." Instead, their growls intensified and they started to advance. Carson shifted his weight and swung the gun toward Jack. "Lie down," she yelled. "Now."

They obeyed, in slow motion, their bodies trembling in rebellion until at last they were down, still growling. "Oh, good dogs," Carson said. "Can't waste any more bullets on you. Let's save them for your mother." He pulled her around them, keeping her body between him and them, dragging her down the steps and heading for the woods. Rachel saw her truck and only Jeb's legs were visible from behind the tail gate. *If he's dead, it's my fault.* That thought kept circling her mind, numbing her until they reached the tree line and she saw a black truck waiting on the old farm road. As Carson muscled her toward the passenger door, she used her thumb to inch her hair tie out of her pocket onto the ground. Leaving some kind of trail might help Seth find her in time.

The bastard opened the door and shoved her inside. Rachel tried to kick him, hoping to buy herself time to run, but he hit her on the head with the pistol, stunning her for a precious moment. She felt the blood river down her face, and he jumped in behind her, pushing her toward the driver's seat. The keys were already in the ignition. “Drive,” he yelled.

She started the engine. “Where are we going?”

Carson pointed down the rutted road. “To your own personal hell,” he trumpeted, with a manic grin. She put the truck in gear and began to drive down the road, shadowed by over-hanging boughs.

Her last thought was of Seth.

Chapter Twenty-Three

Seth had just stepped inside his front door when the radio strapped to his hip buzzed. He pushed the button, "This is Seth."

At first, only static filled the air. Then Jeb's voice sounded, barely loud enough to hear. "Officer down," he said, his words slurred. "He took Rachel."

Seth pressed on his end, his heart racing. "I'm coming, Jeb. Hang on."

He called Rosie and told her to send everyone with an ambulance and ran for his car. Images filled his head, and he pushed them away, screeching around corners, siren on full blast. Precious minutes passed as he whizzed through the edge of town, and finally, down the road to Rachel's. Racing past an open-mouthed Amos on his tractor, he fishtailed on the turn to her driveway. He could see nothing on his approach, then, as he neared the house, he spied a pair of legs extending from the far rear side of Rachel's truck. Rounding the corner, he saw Jeb splayed on the ground, one arm stretched out, fingers clutching the radio. The dogs lay beside him. Seth parked his car to shield him as much as possible, in case anyone waited to ambush them. He eased out of the door, staying against the car for protection while he checked on him.

Crouching down, he saw with relief the deputy's heart still beat. "Jeb, I'm here."

The deputy's eyes fluttered open. They struggled to focus on his face. "He took her, Seth. He took Rachel."

"Now, you listen to me. We'll find her." He ripped open the other man's jacket, felt a physical jolt of relief when he saw the vest, with four embedded bullets. Grabbing the emergency kit from the car, he used hunks of gauze to slow the blood from the one bullet that had hit below the vest, off to one side. As he did so, he heard the wail of approaching sirens. "You're okay. The bullets in your vest likely broke some ribs, and the other wound is off to the side." He prayed he was right about the extent of the damage.

"He was tall, blond, maybe thirty," Jeb said, fighting to keep his eyes open. "Headed for the woods."

"Which direction?"

His left hand flopped toward the rear field. "Back woods."

"Good man." Standing, Seth called the dogs, patting their heads to reassure them, and put them in his car, windows cracked open, so they'd be safe and out of the way. Spying the ambulance waiting on the drive, he waved an all-clear for them to approach. He saw, with a start, not only had the agents come with Wayne, but people had followed the sirens and were standing by the front gate. The group included Rosie, who had parked halfway up the drive where the ambulance had been.

The ambulance attendants hustled toward the deputy and he briefed them on Jeb's wounds. "Don't worry. We've got him," one of them said, hustling to get him loaded onto the stretcher.

"You folks know Rosie?"

"Yes, Sheriff," the female attendant offered as she worked.

"I'm telling her to go in the ambulance with you. She and Jeb are friends. She can stay with him until his folks can get to the hospital."

"No problem." He called Rosie on his cellphone and asked her to notify Jeb's parents and watched as she climbed out of her car and stood waiting as the ambulance made its way down the drive. Wayne, with foresight, kept the driveway clear of onlookers until the ambulance made its way out, then started up the drive.

He and Kendall arrived to join Seth at the same time. "Bill went to check out the house. Do we know what happened?"

Seth turned to Wayne first. The deputy looked pale. "Your cousin should be fine. He took four bullets in the vest, likely cracked a few ribs, which hurts like the devil. Took one more below the vest, but it's off to the side, so he should be okay. I sent Rosie with him."

"Yes, boss." Wayne gulped, wiping the sweat off his face with one sleeve. "Thanks."

Seth took a deep breath. "Here's what we know. The suspect is a tall, blond male, approximately thirty years of age. He took Rachel in that direction." He pointed. "Wayne, you know these woods. Take Kendall and search the high side. Bill and I will take the other side of the farm road. What we're looking for are recent tire tracks. He can't have dragged her along too far on foot. He has to have been parked on one of these back roads." They split apart and then he called out, "Don't go more than a mile in. That's as far as he could have made it on foot in this short amount of time."

Bill hustled to keep up as they headed toward the cover of trees. "We don't have to stay in pairs. We could cover more ground."

Seth tried not to think about how much time Rachel might have and chose to respond instead. “A single person can get lost in a heartbeat up here. The forest is dense, and it goes on for thousands of acres.”

They searched along the dirt road for twenty minutes before his radio crackled. “Think we found it, boss,” Wayne said. “New tracks in the grass and it looks like Rachel might have thrown that fuzzy thing she wears around her hair on the ground.”

“On our way,” Seth said, gesturing for Bill to join him as he switched direction. “Are you about level with Hooky’s house?”

“Just past it, Seth.”

He puffed out a breath. “Can you tell which way the truck was headed?”

“Deeper into the woods.”

Seth swallowed his surprise. “Why would he head deeper into the woods?”

Bill shook his head, struggling to keep up. “Doesn’t make sense. He should be heading for the open road.”

In a few minutes, they caught up with the other two. Seth inspected the tracks the deputy pointed toward. “Wayne’s right. This guy’s headed into deep cover.”

“Why the hell would a stranger do that?” Bill asked. “Progress would be slow, and you know the area better than he does.”

Seth could think of a few really bad reasons someone would do such a thing, mostly scenarios based on a last stand, a final gesture. *Think, damn it, think. Where the hell would he take her around here?*

“We need to regroup,” he said, heading away from

the direction the tracks headed.

"She may not have much time," Kendall said.

He whirled toward her. "Do you think I don't know that?" Taking a deep breath, he apologized. "We need more ammunition and a decent truck to proceed. That road gets pretty rough."

As they started back to the house, his phone rang and he answered. "Sheriff Talbot."

"Well, Sheriff, I have to say, it's a real pleasure to make your acquaintance."

He made a halting gesture to the others and put the caller on speaker. "Who the hell are you?"

"I'm your worst nightmare."

"Oh, I doubt that," he responded. "You just ran back to the city, like the chicken shit you are." He put a finger to his lips, to warn Wayne to be quiet.

"You'll never find me, you back country loser."

"Why would I want to?"

A snigger sounded. "Don't you want to see your girlfriend sliced into pieces and tied up like a ribbon?"

"You're going a little off-script, aren't you? You used a gun. Your precious mentor wouldn't approve."

Now, his sputter of outrage almost made him sound like a girl. "I'm more than he could have ever hoped to be."

"Oh, I don't know. He was pretty smart, I hear. And I'm not even sure you have Rachel. I think she escaped. She's smarter than her father."

He heard a crash and the sound of a struggle and held his breath, hoping he hadn't pushed him too far. "Why don't you say goodbye to your brilliant slut, then." There was a moment of silence, then he heard Rachel's voice. "Don't forget what I told you Monday night," she said, her breath wheezing. He heard the man shriek, then the sound of someone falling. In a moment, he came back on the phone. "I am your fucking master," he screamed. "Don't you forget it." Then came dead air, prompting a jolt of fear.

Seth's mind scrambled with her words. "Wayne, run ahead and get Rachel's asthma puffer. It's in the drawer beside the refrigerator." The deputy took off like a shot, looking like the track champion he'd been in high school. Seth strode back toward the house, waving for the others to follow. When they began to talk, he shushed them. "She was trying to tell me something. Let me think." He ran over all the things they'd talked about that night, then, in frustration, started again. The case, her dogs, her mother, Jeb's house…his mind caught hold. Wayne trotted back across the lawn toward them as Seth had a thought. "Wayne, Rachel told me about the house Jeb's building. Where exactly is it?"

"On my grandma's back acreage. He has ten acres there."

"Can you get access to it on this road?"

He nodded. "Takes a few minutes longer than the main road, but sure you can."

"Are you certain that's where they're headed?" Kendall appeared doubtful. "Why would he choose there?"

"I think he always planned to shoot Jeb. The house is only half done, and Jeb's the only one who ever goes there. It's the perfect spot." Seth pulled out his keys. "We're taking Rachel's truck. She gave me her keys in case we needed it."

"We need more ammunition," Bill suggested.

Stalking over, Seth used a key to unlock the long toolbox in the truck bed. Several rifles shared space with dozens of boxes of ammunition. "I prepared this a few days ago, just in case."

"Told you he was a boy scout," Bill quipped. "I'm good with my pistol. You guys help yourselves." Kendra, Seth, and Wayne grabbed a rifle each, loading and grabbing a box of shells. "Wayne, you're in back," Seth directed. "Stay alert. Vests on, everyone?"

All three nodded. They climbed into the truck, Seth driving and Wayne sitting down, his back against the cab. They drove in near silence for the first four miles, bumping along the rutted path. As they advanced, Wayne leaned in the window and advised him they were getting pretty close and the thick cover of trees would run out soon. Seth pulled the truck over and stepped out to peek through the branches. A half-built log house nestled on the upwards slope with a black pickup parked in front.

I'm coming, Rachel.

He whispered, "Wayne's with me. You two circle around to the back. I can see a light on in the center room. It looks like the only room with walls." The other two disappeared into the cover of the trees, heading uphill.

"Stay right beside me," he said to Wayne. "If he swings a gun toward you, shoot him." The boy was an excellent shot, but he couldn't afford to hesitate.

"Yes, Seth."

They crept forward, and as they inched closer, they could hear a voice. "They'll read my name on every front page in the country. I'm the man who carried out Mark's plan, then became more famous than he did."

Seth heard Rachel answer and her voice became the best gift he'd ever received. "How do you plan to do that?" she wheezed, pushing the words out.

We're here. You're not alone. Just keep him talking. He wished she could hear his thoughts. Instead, he halted Wayne with a gesture and edged up the porch stairs to plant himself against one side of the door opening. After checking to make sure they were clear, he waved Wayne up to the other side. "I'm high, you're low," he whispered to Wayne, then they swept inside, each covering the other. As they advanced, all they heard was a torrent of shouted words. Seth knew they were out of time and kicked the door open, gun raised and ready. He felt Wayne move in behind him, then fan off to the right.

Rachel sat bound in a wooden chair, bloody, but conscious. Once he established that, he focused on the man who stood beside her, a knife to her throat. Carson Gale looked absurdly well-dressed for a psychotic killer, in dress pants and a V-neck sweater. The only giveaway, besides some blood spatters, was the manic glee in his eyes. "You must be smarter than you look, Sheriff."

"Must be." Seth could see the agents had moved into a rear position to help, but were waiting for his next move. "How about you let the woman go?"

He gave a caricature of a grin. "Oh, no. You're going to hurt her feelings, talking like that. Why don't you call her your lady love?" He yanked Rachel's hair, pulling her head back. "Or your whore, to be more accurate."

Seth smiled. "She's worth a million bucks, compared to a piece of scum like you." It happened almost in slow motion then; distracted, the madman lifted the blade mere inches away from her neck and pivoted one step toward them, providing a clear target for just a split second. Seth and Wayne shot in unison, hitting center mass with a pair of shots. There was a stunned pause, and then the murderer fell like a giant oak, banging into the floor hard enough to make it tremble. Kendall reached him first, kicking the knife away, then pinning his arms, just in case. The prevention was all for naught. That bastard would never kill another woman now.

Turning to Rachel with relief, Seth took the folding knife from his pocket to cut the ropes binding her. "I knew you'd come," she said, her voice breaking.

"You gave us the clues we needed. Smart lady." He stroked her hair. "Wayne, do you have—"

Wayne pulled the puffer from his back pocket. "Here, Rachel."

She took a long pull, her hand shaking. "This is a full-service rescue, I see." She tried to smile and a single tear made its way down her cheek.

Bill stood over the body. "Carson Gale. Told you he was hinky," he said to his partner.

Kendall shook her head. "I'll never live this one down."

Chapter Twenty-Four

Seth activated his radio and called for an ambulance to check Rachel out and the coroner for the suspect's body. Then he crouched beside Rachel. "Want to tell me how he got the drop on Jeb?"

"It was my fault," she said, her voice trembling. "I left the dog food in the truck, and Jeb said he'd fetch it for me. When he didn't return, I looked and Gale got the drop on me. I never heard a thing. I guess he ambushed Jeb while I was making sandwiches in the kitchen."

"We found his gun. It has a silencer," Kendall said.

Rachel started to cry. "Did he kill Jeb?"

He leaned down to hug her. "Jeb's going to be okay. The vest caught most of it. He had one bullet down by his hip. They're removing as we speak."

A smile worked its way through her tears. "Are my dogs okay?"

"I locked them in my car. They're fine."

Bill made his way to her side. "Carson was a senior at the university when your father was arrested. And we just received a text. The date listed as the day your father died was incorrect in the files we were given. The day the first victim disappeared was the tenth anniversary of your father's death."

Rachel looked stunned. "I never thought about the exact day he died. I just felt happy he was gone." She started to shiver, and Seth put his jacket around her shoulders as he heard the wail of the approaching ambulance.

Thc attendants checked her out, cleaning up the head wound and making sure the inhaler Wayne provided had controlled her asthma. The female attendant turned to Seth. "I think she's fine, Sheriff, as long as she has someone to stay with her tonight, just to be on the safe side."

"She certainly does. That won't be a problem." He reached out to take her hand. "Any objections?"

She shook her head.

The agents finished taking the necessary pictures of the scene, and the body was removed. They watched the grisly procession in silence. "Jeb will have quite a story to go with his new house," Seth said, when they were gone.

"I hope he won't think it's bad luck now," Rachel answered.

He shook his head. "The best luck ever, you mean. The good guys won, after all."

"True."

Turning to Bill and Kendall, he said, "Thanks for your help. Let's all go and see Jeb."

The group made quite a caravan, heading back to the main road where crowds of people waited at the end of Rachel's drive. They parked, and Seth and the agents climbed out and made a brief statement. Rachel stayed in the car, only waving to comfort Amos and Edith who stood waiting, their faces full of concern.

When they arrived at the hospital, the nurse told them Jeb had just been out of surgery an hour or so, but had done very well. They said he could only see one person at a time, because Rosie was already in there.

Seth left the others in the waiting room and opened the door to find Rosie sitting in a bedside chair, her hand resting in Jeb's. She jerked it away when Seth entered. He struggled to keep the surprise from his face. "The nurse tells me you're doing much better."

"Yes, Sheriff. Still a little groggy, though." His expression darkened. "I'm so sorry."

Seth shook his head. "You've got nothing to feel sorry about, Jeb. You did your best."

"I never thought to look under the truck, but I should have."

The picture became clearer. "He grabbed your ankle?"

"Yes. I lost my balance and went down, hard. Tried to get to my gun, but he just whipped upright and started shooting, point blank."

The town council had thought the vests were a waste of the town's money, but he felt grateful for them now. "Thank goodness for the vest. Right, son?"

He sighed. "Damn straight, Seth."

"Well, the whole gang is outside, concerned about you. And I know your parents are on their way. It'll be a wonderful thing to give them good news."

"They said Rachel is okay."

He nodded. "Lots of blessings there, too. She has a bump and cut on her head, but that's about it." Smiling, he rose. "I'm going to send your cousin in. I'll check back later."

Seth found the others milling around in the waiting room, impatient for news. He filled them in. As they took turns visiting for a few minutes, he whispered to Rachel. "He was holding hands with Rosie."

She looked surprised, then thoughtful. "He said he had a girl in mind when he started building the house. Apparently, she was a little older than him, but he'd loved her as long as he remembered. I just didn't realize it was Rosie."

"I know. I never saw that one coming, either."

An hour later, Jeb's parents appeared, rushing through the automatic doors of the hospital, their expressions born of panic. Seth leapt up with words of reassurance, feeling inadequate when Jeb's mother burst into sobs of relief. He knew the best thing to calm her would be to let her see her son, so he herded them to Jeb's room. After a few minutes, Rosie came out. "Thought I'd let him visit with his parents for a while." She blushed.

"Have you had some food?"

She shook her head. "I guess they're going to make us leave, anyway. Visiting hours are almost over and only immediate family are allowed at night." Looking over at Rachel, she smiled. "I'm so glad you're okay. I'm Rosie, by the way. Nice to meet you."

Rachel smiled in return. "Thank you for staying with Jeb."

The younger woman murmured, "No problem."

After checking back in with Jeb and his parents, Seth shepherded the whole gang out to the parking lot. Since most of their vehicles were at Rachel's, they agreed to head there for some fried chicken and beer to celebrate. Rachel and Rosie sat in the front of the truck with him and the others piled into the back. They made quite an impression picking up the chicken at Momma's, with everyone honking hello or even coming up to the truck at the drive-through. Apparently, the story of Carson Gale's demise had spread through town.

Wayne and Seth loaded a few cases of beer at the local quick stop, and they headed for Rachel's. The deputies on duty reported a quiet night thus far, with lots of people out celebrating their success.

The dogs greeted them, happy to escape the car and ecstatic with all the company. Even Bill managed a ginger pat on their heads before he scuttled to the opposite side of the room. They all ate too much, even Rachel, and then eventually settled all over the den.

Rachel tapped a pen on her can of beer to get everyone's attention. "I want to thank everyone for their hard work on this case. I couldn't have asked for a better support system." Her words were met with cheers, which made her blush. Shortly afterward, people started to peel away, exhausted and ready for rest. Seth saw them out.

"Aren't you supposed to write a report or something?"

Seth realized, in shock, he had just assumed he would always be staying at her side from now on. "We're going to meet at the station and do reports in the morning. You'll have to come along to give your version of events." He ran a hand through his hair. "Is it okay if I stay?"

She looked surprised. "I figured you would." Then she paused. "I'm not sure exactly how this is going to work out for us, but I do want you to stay. Is that enough for now?"

"More than enough." He moved in, wrapping his arms around her. "Shower and bed sound good?"

"Definitely."

****

At six a.m., she woke up, wide-awake, a good thing because she remembered Seth had no clean clothes. She snuck them into the washer for a quick load as he snored. By the time she threw them in the dryer, he'd begun to stir. "Where are you?" he called from the bedroom.

"Making breakfast."

There was a pause, then, "Somebody stole my clothes."

She chuckled. "They need a few more minutes in the dryer." *Is this what carefree feels like?* Looking up, she saw him standing in the open door, buck naked. *Oh, my. Now, there's a compelling sight.*

"How come you got up so early?"

"It's after seven. For me, that's way past lazy." She left the sizzling bacon for a moment and walked over to give him a kiss. He kept her there for three or four more, then she returned to the stove, putting the bacon inside the oven to keep warm, while she scrambled eggs and made some toast.

"Look at you, all domestic and everything," he teased.

Rachel laughed. "Better look quick. It might never happen again." As embarrassing as it was, she found she liked cooking for him when it was her idea and not some archaic dictate.

He walked over to check the dryer, pulling out his clothes.

"Are they dry?"

He shrugged. "Close enough." He stood right there and dressed, stepping around the dogs.

They ate a full breakfast and let it settle while they

walked with the dogs. No more ducking around the back, her eyes peeled for trouble, she thought with relief. With the dogs relaxing back inside, they made their way to the station. Wayne, Kendall and Bill had arrived just before them and were pouring coffee. Rachel saw Bill whispering to Seth, and Seth nodded and whispered back.

What now? Her paranoia crept up, and she pushed it back as they approached. "We'll sit down to write and compare reports before we head home, but there's something we need to talk about," Bill said.

"Okay," she responded, unsure of what to expect.

"Late yesterday, our inquiry about the death of Peter Smythe came in."

Confused, she looked at Seth. "We caught Carson, right? Why is this other stuff important now?"

Bill patted her arm. "It might be important to you, Rachel. Sit down and let me try and explain." He waited until they were all seated. "Apparently there were some unanswered questions about the death of Peter Smythe. His car accident involved his vehicle going into a pond, but it didn't go very deep and Peter still died of drowning. The coroner felt he might have had some help."

"But why would they close the case then?"

Bill shook his head. "It was never closed. It's still a cold case. The medical examiner considered it a suspicious death and marked the cause of death 'undetermined,' despite pressure to sign off on it."

Reaching over, Seth took her hand. "Rachel, we think maybe Marcus Worth murdered Peter Smythe so he could marry your mother."

"No," she protested. "My mother would have never

married him if he did something so horrible."

"What if she didn't know until she started to suspect him for these other killings? Is it possible she finally put it together and that's what broke her?"

She thought about how upset her mother had always been, looking at Peter's picture and it all started to make sense. "She loved Peter first?"

"Think about the ring," he said. "Lovers exchange engraved rings, not friends."

Bill nodded. "We checked with an old teacher of theirs. Apparently, Peter and your mother were a couple first, then Marcus joined their circle as a friend." He leaned forward. "Old schoolmates commented they didn't know how the friendship worked, because Marcus was clearly jealous of Peter, especially since he had joined the brain trust."

The pieces of the intricate puzzle started to move into place. "The blonde thing," she whispered. "Do you think he was trying to kill the memory of Peter?"

"We've been all over this information, backwards and forwards," Kendall said. "Our best guess is that killing those women was his way of killing both Peter and you, over and over again."

The sheer ferocity of his hatred boggled her. "Why would he despise me? I rarely even spoke to him."

There was a pause, as if nobody could decide who should answer, and then Seth spoke. "Because we think Peter Smythe might be your real father."

Chapter Twenty-Five

Rachel felt dizzy suddenly, and she closed her eyes. Someone pushed a cold drink into her hand, and she sipped it. Easing her eyes open again, she saw Seth's anxious look. "I'm okay." She reached into her purse and took out the puffer, inhaling. "That's a bit of a leap, isn't it?"

"Maybe," Kendall said, "but Jeb saw a resemblance and I agree. If Peter was your father, and both you and he tested high enough for the brain trust and Marcus didn't, that's a double strike his oversized ego couldn't tolerate."

"Do you want to know if he's your father?" Seth squeezed her hand. "Your choice."

"How? Peter's been dead for years."

Kendall cleared her throat. "Thanks to the meticulous work done by the medical examiner, his blood has been preserved all these years, because of his case still being open. All we should have to do is get a cheek swab from you and compare it."

The rush of anxiety made her skin prickle and she swallowed, hard. Her father was dead either way, a murder victim or an infamous murderer. There was no question—discovering he was the former rather than the latter might make a huge difference for the rest of her life. She took a deep breath for courage. "I'm in. Let's do it."

Seth smiled. "Bill has a kit with him. All he has to do is take a swab of the inside of your cheek. Then we just have to wait, but Kendall called in a favor and we should get it back within a week."

Interested in the process, they all watched, which made Rachel feel a little like a lab experiment. The strange thing was, when she looked around the room, she saw a bunch of friends she hadn't had just a few short weeks ago. *How did that happen?*

Later on, while Seth worked, Rachel went to see Jeb in the hospital. His parents took the time to grab some lunch at the cafeteria. "How are you feeling?"

"I'm itching to get out of here if you want me to be honest." He shifted in bed, wincing. "There's not much to do except watch television, and if you don't like game shows or soap operas, you're pretty much out of luck."

"I brought you a book." She handed him a new true crime novel, purchased just this morning, which made his face light up.

"Thanks."

"When do the nursing staff think you'll be released?"

"Tomorrow or the next day. But then, they want me to stay at home for six weeks." Judging by his expression, the thought didn't make him too happy.

"Is your mother going to stay and help out?"

He nodded. "She'll hang out during the day and Rosie said she'd help out at night." The mere thought of it lit his face.

She leaned forward and touched the back of his hand. "I want to thank you for noticing that photograph of Peter looked like me."

He gave a long sigh. “I wasn’t sure they had told you yet. Are you going to take the test to be sure?”

“Just did.”

“I’ll be damned,” he said. “My mom always says life throws you apples and oranges, so you’d better learn how to juggle.”

They laughed. “Never heard that one before, but I like it,” Rachel said.

“I have a good feeling about this, Rachel. I think your whole life is about to change.”

She thought about Seth and what might be riding on the results of the test. “You could be right.” As she rose to leave, she paused, looking at his dear face and smiling. Thoughts of Rosie snuck in. “I think your life is about to change for the better, too, Jeb.” Waving, she headed out.

Rachel found Seth sitting on her steps, the dogs plunked down beside him, tongues lolling. “Everything okay?” she called as she climbed out of the truck, groceries in her arms.

“Yup.” He strolled over to greet her and grabbed the bag, lifting it away from the dogs’ sniffing noses. “I cut out early after the final news conference. Felt like we earned a little down time.”

They went inside, and he popped open a beer while she unpacked the food. “So, you want to be my girlfriend?” he asked.

She turned, arching an eyebrow. “What’s this all about?” she asked.

“Well, we kind of missed what my mother used to call ‘the courting stage,’ didn’t we?”

She laughed. “What, chasing murderers isn’t normal seduction? Are you sure?” Ignoring her jumpy stomach, she continued. "I think we should wait and see what the test says."

He stepped in front of her, rubbing his hands down her arms. "It doesn't matter a damn what the test says, Rachel. Not to me."

She sighed. "It does to me, Seth."

"You like facts, right?"

She nodded, wondering where this was headed.

"Well, most whack-a-doos show their colors in their teens and twenties. Did you know that?"

She rolled her eyes. "Now 'whack-a-doos' is a professional term?"

"Whack-a-doos, psychos, freaks, whatever you want to call them."

"So?"

He smiled. "You're thirty-four. You're way too old to be a whack-a-doo."

"I think you might be a whack-a-doo."

He pointed to her. "You might be right. After all, I'm younger than you."

She realized she'd never asked his age. "By how much?"

"A year or so. So, you may not be a whack-a-doo, but you're a cougar, preying on young, innocent me." He walked over and clasped her waist. "Feel free to prey on me, anytime." When they came up for air, she agreed to be his girlfriend. She still had an out if the news was what she feared.

The following week, life went back to normal, with one exception. Seth now spent all his nights with her. Crimes went back to small theft, traffic citations, and the odd domestic call.

On Monday, Seth forgot the lunch she'd made for

him, and he texted, asking if she could bring it down. When she entered, Kendall and Bill were hanging around Rosie's desk. Rachel felt the air leave her lungs. She greeted them, reaching into her purse and taking a long suck on her inhaler. "Do you have the results?"

Kendall nodded, her expression serious and waved her into Seth's office. He sat on the edge of the desk, gesturing toward the visitor's chair.

"Just tell me," she pleaded. "Get it over with."

"Peter Smythe was your father," Kendall said. The other two broke into grins.

She was too scared to trust her words. "Marcus Worth was not my father?"

Kendall shook her head. "The results were run twice, to be sure. There is no doubt."

Rachel burst into sobs, trying to choke them back with no success. Seth shoved past the others, pulled her to a standing position, and hugged her with one arm, stroking her hair with the other. "Just let it out," he said.

They had a hell of a party that night as soon as work closed down for the day. Everyone who had even a small hand in supporting Rachel through her rough time was invited. Even Edith and Amos hired a babysitter for the first time in years. People spilled out onto the patio; everyone from Jeb on crutches with Rosie to Bill, who danced with Edith and ruffled Amos's protective feathers.

At some point, Seth and Rachel escaped for a moment to themselves. Looking up at the sky full of stars, Seth took a breath of the crisp, night air. "Can I move in?"

"I think you already have," Rachel answered, snuggling under his arm for warmth.

He kissed the top of her head. "I mean officially."

"Okay, Sheriff. Officially, I'm asking you to move in."

"Good." He cleared his throat. "Thought maybe I'd sell my house and buy the Hobart land when it comes up for sale."

"Okay." She could see the future now, their coming years through his eyes.

"That would give us fifty acres for the future. Give us all the room we need for kids and plenty of dogs nobody wants but us." He peered down at her, those blue eyes dancing in the shadows. "Sound good?"

"Sounds perfect."

About the Author:

Dianne McCartney has been writing for fifteen years and has won fifty writing awards in contests across Texas and Oklahoma. She is a long-standing member of the Oklahoma Writers Federation, Inc. and a proud member of the Rose Rock Writers and The Rocky Mountain Fiction Writers. She has been a writing contest judge for the last twelve years.

Her first book, *Just One Night*, was released on April 3, 2019.

Find her at:

http://www.diannemccartney.com

~

Also by Dianne McCartney:

JUST ONE NIGHT